I0621850

LARVA

J.D. HUFF

SEVERED PRESS
HOBART TASMANIA

LARVA

Copyright © 2018 J.D. Huff

WWW.SEVEREDPRESS.COM

All rights reserved. No part of this book may be
reproduced or transmitted in any form or by any
electronic or mechanical means, including
photocopying, recording or by any information and
retrieval system, without the written permission of
the publisher and author, except where permitted by law.
This novel is a work of fiction. Names,
characters, places and incidents are the product of
the author's imagination, or are used fictitiously.
Any resemblance to actual events, locales or persons,
living or dead, is purely coincidental.

ISBN: 978-1-925711-98-1
All rights reserved.

1

The pinpoint of light blended seamlessly into the blanket of stars and other heavenly bodies, drifting into the solar system unnoticed. No reaction was generated in response; there was only perfect silence, perfect isolation, and cold beyond normal endurance. It was nothing more than an insignificant speck against the vast backdrop of the universe.

The silver orb was ancient beyond reckoning, a fact belied by the sheen on its outer skin. Well engineered for its astonishing voyage, it looked like it could have been launched yesterday.

As it neared the G2V star, light struck its surface for the first time in countless eons. The energy provided was utilized to start the charging cycle for the on-board operating system. After some time (the orb was patient, if nothing else), it was able to resume functioning. First, a self-diagnostic.

It made an attempt to locate itself, but was thwarted by the fact that none of the constellations within its viewing capability were entered into its memory system. A new reality became apparent. It had gone off the reservation in a monumental way. The orb was lost.

The good news was that the primary reason for its existence, the payload it was carrying, was still in good condition. Although in stasis for many eternities, the embryo appeared to be viable. Encouraged as an electronic mind could be, the diagnosis continued.

The orb didn't know *where* it was, but it did have the ability to determine *when*. A living being capable of abstract thought would have been astounded at the time that had elapsed since its launch. The sun that was now powering it was not even in existence when this mission began. But its electronic brain had no capability for emotion—it filed the information and continued to evaluate.

Several planets circling in this system were located during the subsequent scan. One of them was worthy of a detailed inspection. The little blue sphere, orbiting third from the sun, began to tick off a pre-programmed set of needs that deemed it as a potentially suitable home for the payload; a life form from the farthest reaches of the universe. This was the back-up plan and the only *raison d'etre* remaining in the orb's digital mind.

The operating system used a sophisticated maneuvering device that could help it make subtle maneuvers. The trajectory changed; it was now approaching earth at 300 miles per second.

Its creators would have been proud of this astonishing durability, but they themselves had no such longevity—their world ceased to exist billions of years ago. The orb was now the oldest thing in the entire Milky Way Galaxy. In fact, there was not one living thing in all existence that remembered the orb, or was in any way aware of its existence. Despite that contrary reality, a successful conclusion to the mission that had been lost from all memory was now within reach.

This technological orphan was not a research vehicle, nor was it launched as a means of communicating with distant life forms. Its creators had a more pragmatic motivation.

The orb was a weapon.

The genetically modified larva nestled inside of it would grow into a monster that was designed to lay waste to a distant enemy world. However, a minor mechanical malfunction during the launch phase changed its destiny in a profound way. The orb missed its original target by a relatively small distance. The resulting consequence was inevitable—its odyssey across the incomprehensible vastness of space began.

In suspended animation for a large portion of the universe's very existence, the embryo was now close to getting a chance at life. The orb prepared to fulfil and complete its mission.

As earth neared, a flurry of calculations was made. Entry into the atmosphere and the subsequent landing on the surface posed a real threat to the embryo. The orb could not mitigate the speed at which it fell once gravity claimed it, a risky but necessary proposition. It's not the fall that kills you; it's the sudden stop at the end. The landing would have to be in water to be survivable. Fortunately, the surface of this planet was seventy percent oceans, lakes and rivers.

Contact with the atmosphere itself was going to generate tremendous heat. In the vacuum of space, the orb had the appearance of doing nothing more than drifting along. In fact, it was eating up distance at a speed of nearly seven hundred thousand miles per hour. That would drop off somewhat in the outer atmosphere, but nonetheless, when it reached the blanket of air wrapped around this little jewel, it was going to generate some serious friction. As long as the outer surface of the orb had not been damaged in space, the material should be able to manage both the friction and the resulting heat. According to the sensory ability of the control system, all was fine. As prepared as an artificial life source could be, the orb entered the final phase before entry.

Alaska, July 17, 1949

Big Tony Hones had depleted both his energy and desire for this particular job. He'd been working for twelve hours straight (not for the first time this week), and the locomotive that he was dismantling could wait. The fact that there was a buyer waiting for it somewhere in the contiguous forty-eight was not his problem. In reality, as supervisor of this motley crew of six, it was his problem. But neither he nor his men could work indefinitely and tomorrow was another day. He put two fingers in his mouth, making an ear piercing whistle.

"Let's call it a day," he yelled, the shed walls amplifying his booming voice.

There was no argument.

Tony soon found himself in Rosie's Bar, the exact place he shouldn't have been on a Wednesday night. He exacerbated that situation by staying way too long and drinking way too much. He knew better, but a little voice kept saying *you deserve this*, and besides that—he was starting to believe that the cute little waitress who flirted with everyone was interested in him, and not just the tip he would leave at the end of the night. This scenario became more viable in his mind as the empties piled up, but when he left at closing time, he left alone.

Despite it being the middle of summer, his work shirt wasn't enough to fight off the cool breeze. Grumbling to himself, he shuffled towards the apartment house where he was staying. Once the work in Anchorage was done, he was going back to Detroit City to find a nice union job in one of the automotive plants. In Michigan, the economy of the Motor City was starting to boom.

He looked up to get a better focus as something caught his attention out of the corner of his eye. Streaking across the dark sky was a glowing object leaving an orange tail behind it as it went. It was bigger, brighter, and lasting much longer than any falling star Tony had ever seen. He stood, watching, marvelling at what he was seeing.

"Is that a *missile?*" His face crinkled as he squinted, trying to improve his focus.

The war had been over for a couple years now. Tony heard that Germany had fired missiles at London (another life-enhancing invention inspired by WW2). But surely not. At least not here in Alaska. Besides, there were no enemies left worth worrying about as far as he knew.

The object and its tail disappeared, and Tony resumed his homeward trek. He started to think about the waitress again, and then about how tired and hung over he would be in the morning.

"Stupid ass," he admonished himself.

The sound of an explosion pulled him from his reverie. Its deep reverberations lasted for several seconds and he thought of the thing he had seen in the sky. Maybe it had been a missile after all. The sound faded and he contemplated finding someone to tell. But who? The streets were empty and town silent. Besides, if someone was shooting at Anchorage, their aim was way off. That one must have landed in the middle of nowhere.

"The hell with it. I'm tired." He stumbled bleary-eyed towards his waiting bed.

Illiamna Lake wasn't well known outside of Alaska, but that didn't diminish the reality of its impressive statistics. At its largest point, it was twenty-two miles wide and seventy-seven miles long. Its total surface area was one thousand square miles and it dropped to almost one thousand feet at its greatest depth. Illiamna was a big lake.

It also had the distinction of being one of those rare places in the world that was rumored to be home to a monster. Like Loch Ness, Illiamna was supposedly inhabited by a nefarious sub-surface creature that would tip over fishing boats and attack unwary swimmers. Of course, nobody had a clear photo of it. No real evidence existed. But locals had a litany of tales that recounted "real-life" sightings and other various contacts.

Ironically, after the "meteor crash" on that July night, those locals were right. Whether they or anyone else knew it or not, Illiamna was home to a monster.

2

The orb survived both entry through the atmosphere and the subsequent crash into the lake. More importantly, so did the embryo. After settling into the sediment on the bottom, preparations to bring the alien life form out of suspended animation began.

The water was near three hundred feet deep here—dark, cold and scarcely oxygenated. But the embryo was of a genetically modified creature that was both tough and adaptable. None of these environment factors would pose a problem. The fact that it could live and mature here in complete obscurity was vital. Initial growth would be slow and dictated by the availability of food sources. Time was needed before it could reveal itself and embark on its mission of destruction. By the standards of this new world, it was now small and vulnerable, incapable of wreaking global carnage.

The orb was ready to implement its final task. A virulent acid incorporated into the inner wall housing would activate once a series of electronic pulses were administered. The acid would destroy the orb, and release the embryo in the process. The embryo had an outer body that could withstand the effects of the acid with no long-term damage. The pain it would feel while exposed to the stuff would help bring it to full consciousness, like a slap on the ass by a delivery room doctor. Then things would get interesting.

The creature, shocked by the sting of the acid bath, gulped a breath of lake water while scooting away from what little remained of the orb.

It was amphibious, and could breathe in a wide variety of environments. In the interests of self-preservation, it continued to do just that.

After the longest gestation period imaginable, the little monster was now self-aware. It didn't comprehend where it was, nor did it even know *what* it was. First instincts were to find a hiding place, and this it did. From under the protruding ledge of the partially buried rock, it hunkered and processed its first sensory inputs.

The frigid, watery environment didn't bother it. The creature was, by human reckoning, cold blooded. It adapted to different environmental temperatures without pain or inconvenience. Anything besides being incinerated or frozen solid was tolerable.

The darkness too was fine, perhaps even preferable. It provided cover, and the creature had vision that could overcome any number of obstacles. It had six eyes spaced across its broad, insectile face, each with different viewing capabilities. It could see fine in the gloom of the deep water. As a matter of fact, it could discern subtle movement even now.

A salmon hovered just above the lake bottom, fanning its fins just enough to remain motionless. The creature didn't know what the fish was, but had already determined one thing in its preliminary musings. It was hungry.

The rows of plates along its elongated body were hinged at the front. As it continued to stare at the fish, those plates began to open and close rhythmically. Inside was a type of bladder, a tough membrane which held the water the plates were now pumping through sinewy, one-way valves. Pressure began to build.

Once it reached critical level, the creature extended a tube from its mouth, a multi-purpose appendage, now set to release the buildup of internal pressure in a very specific way. The creature fine-tuned its aim, then released the pressure in a sudden burst. A shock wave rippled through the water, striking the fish. Stunned, it tipped on its side.

The creature, using its horizontally compressed tail for momentum, swam out towards the helpless salmon. A proboscis flicked out of its tube, piercing the side of the fish, a barbed point impaling it. The little monster scuttled back to its hiding place, already applying enough suction to pull the insides of the salmon into its equivalent of a stomach.

Eating was the first lesson learned.

Malhulik, Alaska (population 38), present day

Jeremy Babineau felt good about his situation. And why not? Summer might be short, but an opportunity had presented itself and he was ready to take advantage.

He was set up on the narrow beach, watching the sun setting over the calm waters of Illiamna Lake. Two folding chairs and a cooler full of beer sat on the fine gravel. Stars were just starting to make an appearance in the fading blue sky—the perfect setting for romance.

Best of all, Myah Cloud, the prettiest girl in Malhulik, sat on chair beside him. A multitude of opportunities danced through his imagination.

"Haven't you finished your beer yet?" he chided, knowing alcohol could grease the gears of romance. At least it was having that effect on him.

Mya gave him a disapproving look. "No. Have you?"

"You betcha." Leaning over, he reached into the cooler for another.

"Don't get wasted."

"Why not?" Jeremy couldn't think of any reason not to. He was already well on his way.

"You'll ruin the night."

Unsure of her meaning, he decided to take it in a way that reinforced his lusty ambitions. "No problem. I'll be fully functional for...whatever. Don't worry."

"Are you functional to watch the sun set? Or maybe have a nice talk?"

"Sure. I'm an ace at all that stuff. Whatcha wanna talk about?" At this moment, Jeremy was oblivious of nature. His focus was on Mya. As she looked out over the water, the soft glow of the setting sun reflecting off her face did indeed make her look very pretty.

"Are you staying here or going back to Anchorage?" she said.

"If you're asking me that," Jeremy said, "it must mean you care."

"Maybe I'm hoping to get rid of you."

"Aw, you want me and you know it." Stumbling to his feet, he took her by the hands.

"What are you doing?"

He tugged. "Come on, stand up. Let's dance on the beach."

She looked concerned. "You're going to fall. I don't want to get all dirty."

He was still pulling. "I won't fall. You can hold me up."

"Not likely," she said, standing with reluctance.

"That's better." Leaning in, he kissed her on the cheek, reeking of beer and cheap cigarettes.

"Stop it." His drunken advances didn't add up to romance as far as she was concerned.

"You know you're the prettiest girl in Alaska?"

She attempted to pull away. "I want to go."

He looked like he had been slapped. "Why? I thought you *wanted* to come out here."

"I wanted to talk," she said. "I wanted a chance to look at the stars while getting to know you better. Not to get mauled. I just got here and you're already grabbing at me."

He tried to process her words and failed. "You're just playing hard to get." He leaned in for another kiss, but she pushed him away.

"I'm going. I don't need this."

He stood mute, transitioning from shock to anger.

"Well, fine. Go then. Who needs you? I sure don't." He didn't believe she would actually follow through with the threat.

She snatched her jacket off the back of the chair as she walked away. Just like that, his plans evaporated.

Jeremy couldn't think of anything coherent to say until she had disappeared into the saplings.

"Son of a bitch!"

The transition from thinking he was going to get lucky to realizing he had just been rejected happened way too quickly.

"Great." He kicked her chair over and stood fuming. "Now what?"

He still had a cooler full of beer and a beautiful beach all to himself. He also had a good buzz going. It was bad, but could be worse.

"Screw it. I can have fun without you." He retrieved his open can, taking a good chug. Then, in an act completely devoid of environmental awareness, he tossed it out into the lake. From out over the water came the sound of an immediate secondary splash. He looked towards the source through alcohol blurred eyes. He could see the surface turbulence caused by whatever he had spooked.

"God, that's a big fish." The idea of getting his fishing gear and casting out from the shore occurred to him. Why not? Fishing and drinking wasn't the worst idea a man ever came up with.

He pointed out over the water. "You wait right there. I'll be back with a little something you're going to like."

The calm water bulged for an instant as the monster broke the surface right at the shore.

"Shit!" Jeremy tried to run but succeeded in losing his balance instead. Sprawled on the sand, afterthoughts of a ruined romantic evening were now gone from of his mind. Survival was all that mattered. The dripping abomination was bigger than his pickup. It came towards him as he stumbled back to his feet.

To Jeremy, it looked like a blend between a millipede, a freight train and an army tank. The outer shell was an ebony nightmare, heavy, reinforced with rows of sharp barbs. The blunt head housed a mouth of sorts, which it opened as it got closer. Something inside of it was moving.

The proboscis shot out of the creature, striking him midsection, penetrating his flesh. The tip was barbed, allowing the creature to pull him towards the water. *Resistance is futile*, Jeremy thought despite the pain, with no idea why. That useless contemplation was his final conscious moment. As tremendous suction was applied, his internal organs and other parts were forced through the tube. The creature pulled its twitching prey into the lake to finish feeding in the safety of the watery environment it knew so well.

Its first attempt at hunting on land was a tremendous success. This could open up all sorts of feeding opportunities. That was good. Finding food in the lake was hit or miss. It needed to feed regularly.

It was due for a growth spurt.

Corporal Aya Chee of the Alaska State Troopers entered the small room, not liking what he saw. He was a trim, thirty-six years old and already had over a decade of service with the organization. The possibility that he had been chosen over other candidates due to his indigenous heritage had occurred to him when the initial offer of employment came; but rather than dwell on it, he chose instead to excel in the job, thus justifying their faith in his abilities. This he accomplished with aplomb, becoming the most trusted trooper in his precinct.

The girl seated there was teary eyed and sobbing—on the edge of hysteria, his instincts told him. That would make the interview more challenging and less productive…as if the tedious drive along the narrow dirt road to get to Malhulik wasn't bad enough. He decided to get right down to business.

"You must be Myah."

She nodded, sniffling.

"You're the one who reported Jeremy missing?"

More nodding.

"You were the last one to see him?"

She had to clear her throat before speaking was possible. "Yes."

"When was that?"

She sighed. "Three nights ago."

"Okay." He was scribbling notes on a pad while she talked. "Where was this?"

"On the beach."

"What beach?"

"On the edge of town. Just five minutes' walk from my house."

"Okay. So, why were the two of you there?"

"He asked me to come. It was like a date, I guess."

"A date?"

She fought back a sob. "Yes."

"So what were you two doing, if you don't mind me asking?"

"He had two chairs set up. We were going to watch the sun set over the lake."

"Sounds like a plan. So what happened?"

A tear ran down her cheek. "He'd been drinking. He just wanted to grab me, you know?"

Corporal Chee had a pretty good idea. He nodded.

"So I got mad and left."

"That's the last time anybody saw him?"

"Yes." Her voice diminished.

"Is that unusual for him?" Alaska was full of odd characters, and sudden disappearances weren't that uncommon.

She nodded.

"What do you think happened?"

"I think...he might have drowned."

Aya didn't see a connection. "So, you two were going for a swim?"

"No. But he might have after I left."

"Why?" Aya knew the water was quite cold even in July.

"He does it a lot. Especially after he's been drinking. He likes it."

This whole premise was thin. Before the police were called, several locals scoured this part of the lake in their boats, finding no signs of Jeremy.

"Are you feeling guilty, Myah? Maybe blaming yourself a little bit for his disappearance?"

She made eye contact. "He'd been drinking too much. I should have made him go home instead of leaving him there."

Aya was feeling good about Jeremy's chances. The kid probably went bush for a couple days just to punish Myah for the rejection, hoping she'd jump to this exact conclusion and feel remorseful as a result. Once he had blown off some steam, he would return on his own accord.

"Can you walk me out to the beach? I'd like to see this spot."

She sniffled, nodding. "I can point you in the right direction, but I don't want to be there right now."

"That's fine," Aya said. "If you're up to it, I'd like to go now."

It wasn't long before he was standing by himself on the fine, grey stone. Myah had refused to get close, so he had given her permission to go back home.

There were still two chairs sitting there, one of them tipped over, along with a cooler full of beer and enough driftwood piled for a decent fire. The ground had been trampled by a proliferation of footwear, undoubtedly from the same folks who searched the lake for his body. Hard to make sense out of any of it.

"Swimming is out," Aya said to himself. If the kid had gone in, he would have slipped out of his clothes first, and they weren't here. Foul play in a village of less than forty people wasn't impossible, but seemed unlikely. So that pointed him back to his original conclusion. The kid was hiding out for a few days. He would be back safe and sound any moment now.

It was time to wrap this up and get back to Anchorage.

Later that night, the sun set, putting an end to the long summer day. Seizing the opportunity, the full moon took its place as temporary ruler of the sky. While filtered light from gaps between high, wispy clouds glittered on the surface of the water, the Illiamna Lake monster made another appearance. It emerged at the same place where Jeremy had been attacked, lumbering out across the course sand, water dripping from its body.

In full view, it looked like the larva of some gigantic insect, its head blunt and featureless. The body was disconcerting—robust, bulky and ominous, like a military vehicle from the abyss. It was covered with heavy, dark plating. Sharp barbs had emerged along the sides and top of these plates. Numerous small appendages (legs?) ran along the underside of its body in two parallel rows, giving it the ability to move on land. On the back end was a flap like that on a lobster tail. This was for movement when submerged in water.

It stopped, using the different abilities of its eyes to seek out prey. This foray out of the lake was no random venture—the monster was hungry.

It moved off the beach, trundling towards the village. The scrub brush along the edge of the sand was no obstacle; it trampled it flat to the ground. A wooden structure came into view as soon as the monster emerged from the growth, onto the gravel road. It didn't appear to be natural, thus needing further exploration.

The monster moved closer without making a sound. One eye had thermal capabilities, and after some fine tuning, was able to identify two life forms inside the structure. They were eating size and motionless. And that was fine.

The plates began to pivot open and shut, drawing in air, building pressure. The outer portion of the proboscis, where the release ports were located, was adjusted as the creature aimed it at the structure. When the pressure was at its maximum, it was released.

The sound was like someone hitting a gigantic gong with a rubber mallet, a booming vibration of air. The shock wave hit the house at the speed of sound, the windows and closest walls exploded. Splinters of glass and wood flew in all directions. The roof sagged with the sudden lack of support along one side. A loud, shrill screaming came from inside the structure. The monster moved towards it. This had worked very well indeed. Now it was feeding time.

The man inside tried to run off through the gaping hole before the proboscis put an end to his efforts. His wife, unceremoniously abandoned by her life partner, was trapped under some debris and lay there as the creature approached to feast.

It drained both, then snipped them into bite size pieces with the razor sharp beak which covered the proboscis when it wasn't in use. This was double the intake from the previous meal on the beach. It would do for now, but the monster had a metabolism that would speed up, enabling tremendous growth when unlimited food was available. It was at a point in its development where exponential enlargement was possible. It would submerge again until this meal was processed.

It slid back under the water to the safety of the lake. But it would return soon. It had stumbled upon a most excellent food source.

3

"It's the damnedest thing."

Corporal Aya Chee had not expected to be back in Malhulik so soon (if ever). The house before him was, for all intents and purposes, destroyed. Worse—both occupants were missing.

"What is, Bill?" he said.

Sergeant William Taft was his superior, and an expert on explosives. He had been sifting through the rubble, looking for clues as to what had happened. Now he stood amidst the debris, looking flummoxed.

"This wall exploded inwards," the Sergeant replied.

Aya raised his eyebrows. "That means the source came from out here?"

"Must have. If that's true, then we can eliminate all the usual suspects for the cause. No gas leaks from heaters or stoves."

Aya spun in a circle, scanning the ground. "If it came from out here, where are the signs? There's no impact hole, no charring of the ground, no debris thrown from anywhere but the house."

Taft stepped out of what remained of the structure. "I didn't say it was going to make it easier to figure out."

"And the occupants?"

Taft brushed his trousers to remove dust. "There's no sign of them in there."

Aya shook his head. "None at all?"

"There's a little blood on the wood by the bed on the east side. Not much, mind you. But, no bodies."

"Nobody saw or heard any of this?"

Taft stood motionless, waxing reflective as he tried to imagine whatever this had been as it unfolded. "The house was wrecked by the time anybody walked past this morning. A couple people reported hearing something that they described as sounding like loud humming during the night, whatever that means. But no useful details at all."

Aya could imagine what was going to happen next and he wasn't happy about it at all. He did not want to spend the night in Malhulik.

"Tell me about the call you had here the other day," Taft said. "Could it be in any way related to this?"

Aya shook his head. "Naw. Some kid went missing after having a fight with a girl. I think he went bush to punish her, or maybe blow off some steam."

"Has he returned?"

"Apparently not. But I can't see any connection to this."

"Me neither," Taft said. "But if he's gone much longer, we're going to have to take his situation more seriously. How long has he been missing in total?"

"Four days."

"Did you talk to his employer?"

"I did. They haven't seen him either. I think he's fired."

Taft repeated the scan Aya had done, seeing nothing helpful.

"What now, boss?" Aya knew the answer could be trouble for him, but postponing the inevitable wouldn't change the outcome.

"Aya, I want you to stay. Track the kid and bring him back. He's going to be in trouble if he stays out there much longer anyway. I'm going to be here for the rest of the afternoon getting samples to take back at the lab."

"Great," Aya said with limited enthusiasm.

"Two days. I doubt he went far. I'll be back to pick you up. Take whatever supplies you need out of the truck. You can get set up at the school to spend the night. Kids are out for the summer, so…"

Aya could have resented the fact that his superior thought he could magically track people in the woods because he was indigenous, but the reality was, he did have a gift for it. He was always a popular addition to any hunting party.

"I'll talk to the principal and give her the good news." The school was only slightly larger than most of the houses here, but it had a cot in the nurses' room. It would do.

"Unless you get hot on the trail and want to spend the night out under the stars."

Stars and mosquitos, Aya thought. "I'll see if I can get his trail and go from there."

Taft waved him off. "Good hunting."

Aya dumped his stuff beside the cot in the nurse's room at the school. The mattress looked too thin to be comfortable. "Beats a night in the bush," he told himself, although not convinced it was true.

He repacked his bag as lightly as possible. Next stop was the beach, where all this started.

Once there, he spent some time putting himself in Jeremy's shoes. Inexperienced, drunk and pissed off enough to do something stupid—if the kid went into the woods to disappear, which direction would he have taken?

Aya decided to go east. The tree line consisted of smaller growth in that direction. It looked more open, easier to navigate. Carrying his small pack with minimal gear, he wandered off, looking for any signs of Jeremy.

He was three hours in, meandering in a serpentine manner to cover the most ground, before he became convinced that no one had come this way. There were no signs at all. An inebriated kid should have left a noticeable trail.

On the return trip, Aya walked an arrow straight path and cut the travel time in half. When he stepped back onto the beach, it was late afternoon. But it was summer in Alaska and darkness wouldn't fall for quite some time. He decided to go west this time, back into the woods. If the kid was out there, he might be glad to get found. Being lost was one plausible reason why he hadn't returned yet.

Aya repeated his first venture, going three hours in before coming to the same disappointing conclusion. Jeremy hadn't come this way either.

Rather than face the walk back, Aya decided to bed down and spend the night. The idea didn't fill him with dread. Now that he was out here, a night in a natural setting seemed appealing. He found a somewhat sheltered spot under the boughs of a huge evergreen. The branches would keep the dew off, and the bed of needles would be a soft surface to lie on.

He unpacked a thin plastic sheet and spread it over a flat spot. Then, he ate some moose jerky that his uncle had made, munching slowly. At least he had a thought to occupy his mind while winding down towards sleep.

If Jeremy hadn't run off into the woods, where was he?

Aya was up early. Indigenous or not, he felt the aches that came from sleeping on the ground. In his mind, however, he felt rejuvenated. He packed up his simple camp site and began the walk back. He savored the singing birds and all the sounds and smells of nature. Once back in Anchorage, he wouldn't have time or opportunity for any of that.

When he emerged from the woods, he was once again entertaining the idea that Jeremy could have drowned. But if so, why hadn't his body been found? Aya decided to ask the locals to do another, more thorough search of this part of the lake. His body might be tangled up in the plant life along the shore.

He walked past the destroyed house, now encircled by yellow caution tape, wondering if Taft had been able to find any answers about what happened there. Hopefully, the occupants had reappeared, providing information to fill in the blanks.

He turned the corner, walked past a small copse of trees. Aya stopped dead in his tracks, as what remained of the village of Malhulik came into view.

His first impression was that the buildings had all exploded. Splintered remains of the wooden structures were spread over the roadway and in front yards. But there was no smoke, no sign of fire—none of the telltale evidence found after an explosion. It was as if the entire village had been stepped on and crushed by a giant. All around him was total silence.

Overwhelmed to the point where he didn't know what to do next, he started to advance, all senses on full alert. Yesterday it had been a village. Now it was a mangled ghost town. What had happened here? Where was everybody?

His reawakened tracking skills kicked in. He looked down as he walked, and saw a strange set of imprints in the dirt, like parallel rows of small, round pads set close together. His initial thought was that they were from some sort of machine, maybe an ATV of some sort. The pattern was like that from a tracked vehicle, but that couldn't explain what happened here. Aya decided to risk making some noise.

"Hello!"

His voice sounded loud in contrast to the silence around him.

"Anybody here?"

No response, but then he saw movement. A little boy wandered out from behind a mangled home. Aya fought off the urge to run towards him. That might spook him, causing him to bolt.

"Hi there." Aya approached as casually as he knew how.

The boy stood in silence, allowing the officer to close the gap between them.

"I'm Aya. What's your name?" He was in front of him now, crouching down on one knee.

"Denny."

The boy's voice was squeaky soft. In contrast to this disaster, Aya found it tugging at his heartstrings.

"Hi Denny. Nice to meet you."

A single tear traced down the boy's dirty cheek.

"Denny, can you tell me what happened here?"

He shook his head no as his eyes grew wide.

"Did you see anything scary?"

This time, he nodded.

"It's okay. I'm a policeman. You can tell me."

More tears emerged, but no response.

"Is there anybody else still around?"

He shook his head.

"Where did they go?"

A moment of hesitation, then, "The monster eated them up."

Aya fought the urge to react, forcing himself to stay calm. "You saw a monster?"

The boy nodded.

It was an unexpected corner to be backed into. Where to go now? "What did it look like, Denny?"

The boy froze, looking terrified.

"Was it big?"

More nodding.

"Did it…look like a bear?" It was a shot in the dark.

"No."

"Where is it now?"

No response.

"Did you see which way it went?"

He nodded, whispering something Aya couldn't make out.

"I didn't hear you, Denny. Could you say that again?"

"The lake." The boy seemed to be reaching his limit for cooperation.

Aya couldn't help but glance in that direction, as if there was something there to see. "Okay. Listen. How about you and I go looking around to see if we can find anybody else."

The boy seemed to be rooted to the spot, and Aya had bigger problems. Malhulik was notorious for being a dead spot for cell phone coverage. Since Taft had driven the police vehicle back to Anchorage, his only hope for communication with the outside world revolved around the viability of the landlines in the village. He hoped that despite all this damage, the phones would still work.

He scooped Danny into his arms. "Come on, pal. Let's go see what the school looks like." It was the largest, most well-constructed building in the village. Maybe it would still be in good condition. For the moment, it was all that he could think to do.

4

In addition to instinct, the monster had an inherent intelligence which was focused around finding food sources. The village where it had been feeding was now devoid of easy meals. There were two other hamlets on the edge of Illiamna Lake, each slightly larger but significantly more remote than Malhulik. It found and feasted on these two pockets of civilization over the next two consecutive nights. By now, the monster had grown to a size larger than most of the homes it was destroying. This lakeshore foraging had been good, but the sources were now depleted. It was time to leave the water that had been its home to find less limited feeding grounds.

Aya lifted the mug to his lips. Both it and the coffee it held were ice cold. He lowered it back to the desk without taking a sip.

"Tell me again about the tracks you saw."

Aya was starting to feel more like a criminal than a member of the law enforcement team. He tried to readjust his position. Perhaps this chair had seemed comfortable once, but that was long past. As far as Aya was concerned at this point, if he never had another interaction with the FBI, it would be fine with him.

"It was like two sets of pads, running parallel to each other."

There had been two agents conducting the interview, but one had left without explanation. Probably having a nice supper somewhere, Aya supposed.

"Okay, what do you mean by "pads"?"

"They were round, maybe a foot in diameter. There was no deep pattern cut into them, like tread on a tire. They were set somewhere around six feet apart. Like I already said, they were running parallel to each other."

"What did you attribute them to?"

"I don't know. My thought at the time was maybe some sort of all-terrain vehicle."

"What do you mean by that?"

Are you daft or just enjoying my discomfort? Aya kept his reaction to himself, proceeding calmly, even though it wasn't the first go around for these questions. "Like one of those tourist vehicles that can run on snow or dry ground. Something that can run over rocks and uneven surfaces. You know, a tracked vehicle, not something that runs on wheels."

The agent kept scribbling notes, but couldn't supress a sigh. "But you never saw this vehicle?"

"No."

"Or anything else important for that matter?"

Aya was finding it harder to remain poised. "I saw lots of things."

The agent made eye contact. "But nothing that could have been responsible for the damage to the village?"

"No."

"Or any signs of survivors or victims?"

"Just the boy. How is he, by the way?"

"He's with his aunt in Juneau. Physically, he's doing well."

Aya squirmed again. "You haven't asked me anything new for some time now. Are we almost done?"

The agent leaned away from the desk into a more upright posture.

Here it comes, Aya thought. *He's pissed now.*

"Yes, I think we're finished." He extended his hand, which Aya shook in reflex and mild surprise. "Thank you for your time, Corporal. The Alaska State Troopers are a fine organization and we appreciate the cooperation."

This was the moment he had been waiting for, and there was no way he was going to waste it. Aya stood, preparing to leave.

"I would reiterate that you can't talk to anyone about what you saw at Malhulik."

Aya had heard rumors that other villages had suffered the same fate but knew better than to ask. He decided not to dignify the request with a response.

"I've got to pee." With that, he made his exit.

Prince William Sound, three days later.

"Where's the damn whales?" Bob Englund was freezing and his glass was empty.

His wife gave him a withering stare. The deal had been that he wouldn't complain or drink his way through the cruise. He had been in violation of both restrictions from the onset.

"Tell me again why we didn't go to the Caribbean."

She continued to lean out over the railing, scanning the blue waters for any signs of life. "Because I thought this might be the one place in the world where you wouldn't bitch incessantly."

"How's that working out?"

He took pleasure in being miserable and that made things worse. She considered the logistics of chucking him over the railing. In the end, she decided he was too heavy.

"I'm going back in. I need another drink and maybe a nap."

"One leads to the other," she observed.

"Hmm?"

"Just go."

He turned, walking away. He was discombobulated from the onset. Finding the right door on a ship that was just shy of one thousand feet long, while drunk, was not an easy venture.

Sherri Englund, his suffering wife for over forty years, recognized that he was in trouble but was determined not to help. If he drank less, this sort of thing wouldn't be a problem. He wandered off, grumbling as he went. She returned her gaze to the gorgeous view of the Alaskan coast. Whales or not, this was worth the time and effort. It occurred to her that, like this trip, most aspects of her life would be nice—except for the unappealing lout she was attached to. The original love was still there, but the supporting foundation had long since eroded away. Maybe it was time to make a change. She stared out, pondering the implications.

Bob found his way inside the *Azure Paradise*, flagship of the Alaska cruisers, and remembered where the bar was. He weaved along the narrow hall, coming close to bumping into a young couple as they passed. It took all the reserves of decency he had remaining not to say something rude to them, indicating (as far as he was concerned) that the near-miss had been their fault.

A sudden, violent vibration brought all Bob's pretense of sobriety to a crashing halt. The sound of a gigantic gong being rung assaulted his ears and he toppled onto the floor. He was too embarrassed not to get angry, and too angry to contemplate the implications of losing his composure.

"What the hell was that?" He squirmed into a kneeling position, a scathing glare warning the young man not to offer any assistance.

A second vibration hit them. This time Bob's vision went blurry, his ears rang and his dental work felt like it was coming loose. He landed face-first, flat on the floor again. The good news, to his reckoning, was that the young couple both fell, joining him there.

The woman was looking at her husband with terror in her eyes. "Do you think we hit an iceberg?" she whispered.

Bob couldn't help but react. "Iceberg my ass. Thank you, James Cameron, for contributing to the dumbing down of America."

"Hey!" The young man, who Bob now noticed had very broad shoulders, came to his wife's defense. "There's no need to be rude."

Bob was still making no attempt to stand. "Relax. We probably ran into one of those stupid whales that my wife wanted to see."

The monster had attacked twice under water. There were results, but the damage to this gargantuan vessel wasn't enough to incapacitate it. It rose up, breaking the surface. Plates began to move, building pressure from air instead of water, while its proboscis aimed at the weakened area of the hull. This feeding opportunity was too good to give up on.

The pressure reached a critical stage and released. A shock wave flew across the water, rippling the surface as it went. It struck the ship like an enormous hammer, sending phenomenal vibrations through the entire structure. Welds cracked, rivets snapped, and a huge metal plate along the side tore loose, allowing a wall of water to gush into the hull. The monster analysed the damage, concluding that it was terminal. Next came figuring out the best method for feeding on the numerous creatures inside, their presence detected by the heat signature each gave off.

The monster prepared to enjoy a buffet that would spur on another growth spurt. This one would be quite significant.

"We must have hit *something*!" the Captain screamed, wiping blood off his forehead with the back of his hand. He had fallen hard. Every person on the bridge had gone down, but some more gracefully than he had.

"Nothing on radar, sonar or visual, sir," the pilot responded, scrambling back to his feet. "It was more like something hit us."

"Put out a distress call. I heard metal tearing, which means we're taking on water."

"Yes, sir."

The Captain grabbed the microphone that reached the radios all crew members carried. "This is the Captain! Somebody get me a damage report! Now!"

The question was how to react? There were over three thousand souls on board including the crew. At this moment, they were all relying on him to make the right decision. A red light started to blink on the communication panel. The Captain punched the switch without hesitation.

"This is the Captain."

"Sir, this is Chief Steward Harris."

"Talk to me, Harris. What have you got?"

"I'm looking over the rail on the port side. This side of the ship…is gone."

The information didn't compute. "What do you mean, gone?"

"There's a gigantic hole. Some of the metal plating just peeled away. There's nothing to stop the water from rushing in. We're going to sink, and soon."

The Captain was too stunned to respond.

"Sir, are you there? Did you hear me?"

"How much time do we have?"

There was a short pause. "Not much."

The Captain walked over to the controls, looking at the readings.

"My God. We're already listing three degrees." Three degrees was survivable, not yet even noticeable by their guests—but when it happened this fast, there would be no happy ending.

"What should we do, sir?" the pilot asked.

The Captain collected himself as best he could. Despite his absolute horror at what was transpiring, he was also somewhat in awe. When he spoke again, his voice was subdued. "We'll be under water in twenty minutes. There's no time."

"Sir?"

"Sound the general alarm." His face was now old and haggard. "It's every man for himself."

5

The USCGC Toklat, an Alaskan Coast Guard cutter, was twenty miles away when the distress call came in. Captain Anne Duparte was on the bridge, responding the only way she knew how—decisively.

"Flank speed. Sound the general alarm. Get us there, Ensign. Let's help those people."

"Yes, Captain." The hairs stood up on his arm. He had never heard the Captain call for flank speed before.

The engines were already responding. Running flat out would push the ship past thirty knots. That would get them alongside in forty minutes, hopefully before the hull damage being reported could have a severe effect on the cruise ship.

"Call Lieutenant Silvers up here. And get me Eielson AFB on the horn. I want to know what they have in the air."

She picked up the powerful binoculars, looking out over the horizon. It was a clear, calm day, but all she could see now was a fuzzy brown blur that represented the coast.

"Petty Officer Kowalski!"

The young man almost tripped himself as he ran over.

"Yes, Captain?" he asked, wide-eyed in anticipation.

"This is important, Kowalski. Do you understand?"

"Yes, Captain."

"I need a coffee. Large. One cream, two sugars. Got it?"

"Yes, Captain!"

"Stat."

He scrambled off.

"Ensign Platt. Bring up the *Azure Paradise.* Let's see what we're going to be dealing with."

"Yes, Captain." The slender young man sat at a nearby work station, his fingers flying over the keyboard.

"That's it." She leaned over his shoulder to get a better view of the screen. She was interested in numbers of people on board. According to the computer, between passengers and crew, sold out capacity would be close to three thousand five hundred souls. She stood upright, musing over the implications.

"That's all I need, Ensign. Thank you."

"Aye, Captain."

That many people would be way past the ability of her ship to save. She said a quick prayer that the damage would be minimal.

"Where's that coffee?"

Sherri Englund leaned over the railing, staring at the mangled side of the ship. She had no idea how this had happened, but one thing did seem obvious. This kind of damage was beyond repair and would be terminal for the ship. They were going to sink into these frigid waters within view of the beautiful shoreline and there was nothing that could stop it. A number of crew members were going through the preliminary procedures for launching the lifeboats, she noticed. The ship was already leaning to the point where they were having issues swinging the smaller boats into launch position. She was beginning to doubt that they would get any in the water. *So this is where it all ends*, she thought in a calm manner.

Perhaps the normal thing to do would be to run off in search of her husband so they could be together. She found that she had no desire to do that. Instead, she returned her gaze and attention to the rugged beauty of the Alaskan coast. Surely there were worse places and ways to meet your end. That was when movement in the water caught her attention and she saw the monster rise to the surface.

She gasped in shock and surprise. It was a disgusting, abomination of a thing. It remained motionless a short distance away, waiting and watching as the boat went through its inevitable death throes. She had never seen anything resembling it before. It was not a whale, although the size was perhaps similar to a big one. Why was it here? And what was it waiting for?

The once peaceful feeling of submission to her fate evaporated. What replaced it was a rising dread caused by the appearance of this creature. As much as she wanted to, she couldn't turn her eyes away from its disturbing visage.

People were now appearing on the deck, most transitioning from anger to panic as the reality of their situation became clear. None had yet seen the monster, as far as Sherri could tell from their incoherent ramblings. Perhaps that was just as well.

Captain Duparte trained the binoculars on the area that was their destination. This time she was rewarded with a blurry view of the *Azure Paradise*. Details were hazy, but one thing was obvious. She was in a lot of trouble.

"Good Lord." She lowered the binoculars. Several of the crewmembers with her on the bridge had heard her reaction and were now glancing her way. "Lieutenant Silvers?"

"Yes Captain?"

"Prepare for a worst case scenario. That ship is going to capsize before we can reach her. We'll be looking for people in the water."

The color drained from his face. "How is that possible?"

The Captain ignored his question, taking it as rhetorical. There was no time for speculation. "Get the Zodiacs ready for immediate launch once we arrive. Prepare the crew."

"Yes, Captain."

She would have preferred more strength in the tenor of his voice. "This is what we train for, Lieutenant. Get your people in position."

He snapped a salute, walking off briskly. *Better*, she thought. "Get me Eielson again. I need to talk to the base commander."

The communications officer made an immediate response. They all had adrenalin flowing in their veins now.

Eielson AFB dispatched an F-15 and two rescue choppers to the site of the distressed ship. The fighter jet, capable of Mach 2 speeds, measured its ETA in minutes. The choppers would be measured in hours. Although they didn't realize it yet, they were going to be way too late.

The jet ramped up to maximum speed at the behest of the base commander. Once achieved, it would eat up distance at a rate of one mile every two seconds. Eielson was three hundred miles away, but the F-15E Strike Eagle could do that in less time than it took to heat up a can of soup. The twin engines roared as the after-burners lit up. The thunder it created added to the impressive display of military technology. The problem was the jet could only observe once it arrived. It was in no way configured to assist in rescue attempts.

At least the updated info it could provide would be helpful in setting up more comprehensive plans to deal with this situation. The pilot, First Lieutenant Thomas Nelson, imagined tourists waving at him from the deck of the ship as he did a close fly-by. In this assumption, he was very wrong.

Captain Duparte tried not to let her frustration show to the crew. This was taking way too long. They were close enough now for the *Azure Paradise* to be seen with the naked eye. It had already rolled over onto its side. The crew, seeing this, had become very quiet.

The communications officer stood upright, walking away from his work station, as if in a dream.

"Is there a problem, Ensign?" the Captain asked in an icy tone. This was not the time for any of them to start losing their composure.

"Do you see that?" he asked.

She refocused. *What the hell?* "Hand me the binoculars." She fine-tuned her aim, refocusing for clarity. Roiling in the water by the side of the sinking vessel was some sort of large, black creature. At first she thought it must be an orca, but the longer she looked, the more horrified she became.

"Captain," the communications officer said, "what is it?"

In complete disbelief, she watched the black abomination snatch a survivor from the water. She lowered the binoculars, feeling like someone had just punched her.

"Captain?"

She ignored the inquiry. What to do? Her ingrained response demanded an immediate decision. The Toklat had several weapons systems, but none had the kind of pinpoint accuracy needed to shoot amongst the floating survivors, guaranteeing no collateral damage.

"Get Lieutenant Larson on the deck! Tell him to bring his 50 cal. with him! Now!"

Larson had trained to be a sniper. He was the best chance to hit whatever that creature was without striking a survivor.

"What do I tell him, Captain?"

"Tell him to shoot that damn thing!"

Nelson reduced power, dropping his fighter down. The coast was fast approaching and he needed to get close for a detailed inspection of the *Azure Paradise*. He put the F-15 in a parallel course to the shore, banking it just enough to get an unimpeded view. What he saw astonished and horrified him. Only his training kept him calm in response.

"Eielson, Falcon three-niner-seven, over."

"Go ahead, three-niner-seven."

"I have eyes on the ship. Be advised, she has already capsized, over."

The radio grew silent. Nelson had already gone by, turning to line up for another, slower pass.

"Please repeat, three-niner-seven."

"The ship has capsized. She is going to be under in minutes."

More silence.

"Eielson, also be advised, I see the Toklat approaching. Repeat, Toklat is on site. Hopefully, she can initiate rescue procedures in a big hurry."

"Roger. How close to shore is the cruise ship? Could local search and rescue be of assistance?"

Nelson had to think about that one. "They'd better hurry."

"Roger. We'll make the call."

Nelson squinted as if to sharpen his 20/20 vision even further. "Base—be advised that I have eyes on something in the water. It's right beside the ship."

"Three-niner-seven, could you elaborate?"

"My God. I think it's alive. And...I think it's attacking the survivors." His fighter was carrying ammo for his guns, but they would do more harm than good in a situation like this.

"Can you engage?"

"Negative, base. Survivors are too close." This was the most frustrating feeling he'd ever had. "Do you have an ETA for the choppers?"

Three-niner-seven, be advised ETA is still over an hour."

That wasn't going to work.

It was up to the Toklat now.

Captain Duparte was on the deck. Lieutenant Larson was setting up his bipod, taking position.

"Shoot the damn thing, Dick." They had watched it devour three more swimmers. If this got any worse, she was going to engage it with the big guns, consequences or not.

"Aye, Captain." His training and instincts kicked in as he took aim.

The .50 cal made a satisfying roar when it fired. The Captain swore she saw the bullet strike the side of the monster. It turned towards them.

"Captain?"

"Fire at will, Lieutenant. You're doing just fine. Give it hell."

He ejected the spent shell, preparing to fire again. This time he aimed for the face of the thing.

"Eat this," he said as he applied pressure to the trigger.

The monster felt the first bullet strike. It was a heavy load with scorching velocity, but the plating on its side wasn't even scratched. Nonetheless, it had been attacked. This dictated a response. In its enthusiasm to eat, the approaching ship hadn't even been noticed. This had been a mistake that couldn't be repeated. Evasive action wasn't yet required based on the limited damaged the direct hit had made. Its plates began to build up air pressure.

"Captain?"

"I see it." The creature was puffing itself up as if to appear bigger. Maybe it thought it was being intimidating. "Shoot it in the head again, Lieutenant. I don't think it likes it." The next shot was a good one, striking the transparent plating in front of one eye.

The creature released its attack.

They both saw it coming; a shimmering distortion racing towards them. The hammer of pressurized air flew across the water. Standing stoically, the Captain casually crossed her arms in defiance. "I don't care for the look of that," she said.

Lieutenant Larson was less eloquent with his final words. "Shit."

The wave hit the ship dead on. Unprotected from the impact, they both flew through the air from the impact, bodies turned to jelly. The ship rocked, but the hull held together. Glass from all windows on that side of the ship exploded inward in a shower of shards.

As this transpired, the monster began to load up for another shot.

There was chaos on the bridge. The crew scrambled to regain their footing, exchanging confused glances.

The monster had narrowed the tip of its proboscis before releasing the next barrage. This time, the built-up pressure wasn't a hammer—it was a spear.

The focused energy of this shot punched through the hull with ease. The Toklat rocked under the impact, most surviving crew members once again thrown to the floor. Water rushed in through the gaping hole. She was going to suffer the same fate as the *Azure Paradise*.

Nelson had seen it all happen. "Eielson, Toklat is under attack! Repeat, Toklat is under attack! That thing is firing at it. I see severe hull damage, over!"

The response came without hesitation. "Three-niner-seven, you are clear to engage. Repeat; you are clear to engage."

It was music to the pilot's ears. He punched the throttle, banking into a sharp turn. He flipped the switch that would enable firing of his guns. This situation was going to change if he had anything to say about it.

The F-15 finished its turn and lined up for a strafing run. The Vulcan 20mm Gatling rotary gun could fire at a maximum rate of 7,200 rounds per minute. It was a fine way of saying hello to your enemies. Although not capable of pinpoint accuracy, with that many shots in the air, hitting the target wasn't going to be too challenging. Saying a quick prayer for those in the water that still survived, Nelson slid his finger over the trigger.

The bullets hit the water with tremendous velocity, churning the surface, shooting froth into the air. They struck in a line, raking over the creature, scoring numerous hits.

"How'd you like that, asshole?" It wasn't the most professional thing to say, but under the circumstances, nobody would blame him. The fighter flew past, but before Nelson could initiate a turn to line up for another attack, he hit the worst turbulence he had ever encountered. It felt like his jet had flown into an invisible wall. The consequences were disastrous.

Both engines flamed out and the canopy cracked. Instrumentation failed and pieces of the planes' frame rattled loose. It began to fall, spinning out of control in a death spiral. Nelson had a brief moment to make his last decision as pilot of the jet. He pulled the eject lever, surprised when it worked. There was no time to contemplate the landing in the icy water—at least he had gained a few more moments of life.

The monster watched as this adversary suffered the effects of its attack. The jet arced downwards, striking the ocean, parts flying in all directions. The resulting debris settled into the water and began to sink.

The bullets that struck it had hurt, perhaps causing bruising under the heavy plates, although there didn't seem to be any permanent damage done. It hadn't noticed the billowing parachute that was dropping out of the sky. All threats now seemed to be eliminated.

It was time to resume eating.

6

"Mr. President?"

The man at the head of the table looked over, an unhappy expression displayed for all to see.

"What is it, Andrew?" His voice was strained.

"Sir, my apologies. I need to speak to you privately."

He scowled. "Folks, sorry about this. I'll be right back." He stood while growling.

This isn't going to be much fun, Andrew thought. The President was not hard to read as far as his emotional status was concerned.

"For God's sake, Andrew. These preliminary talks are crucial. I thought I left orders not to be interrupted. What is so damn important?"

"Sir, our naval and air force commanders are on the way. There is an emergency meeting in ten minutes."

"For what, man? We have a military emergency every day around here."

It was one of the most secure places in the world to have a conversation, but Andrew lowered his voice. "An Air Force F-15 and a Coast Guard Cutter have just been destroyed off the coast of Alaska. They were responding to a distress call from a cruise ship that has also been sunk."

The President's face paled. "Is it the Koreans?"

"We don't know, sir. The situation is still unfolding."

"Two ships *and* a plane? What the hell?"

Was that an actual question? Andrew hesitated, unsure if a response was required.

"Well, come on then," the President said, as he started walking. "And have somebody give my regrets to the delegation. So much for smoothing that over."

Andrew had reservations about how much smoothing the President was capable of. "Yes sir. I'll take care of it."

The President could walk at a surprising rate when he was motivated. He was already pulling away.

"Oh, and Andrew?"

"Yes sir?"

"See if you can rustle me up a cheese omelette. I'm starved and this sounds like it could take a while."

Everyone snapped to attention when POTUS entered the Situation Room.

"Everybody relax. Take a seat."

Expressed sentiments notwithstanding, it was hard to relax when the President was around. He had a way of keeping people off balance.

"Bill, what the hell is going on?"

Only two people on the planet referred to Admiral William Bowles, Commander of the Pacific fleet, as "Bill". The other was his high school sweetheart.

"Mr. President, we have four Raptors from Eielson arriving on scene now. They have a full load of weaponry, including the new two-stage missiles. They also have cameras that can give us a live feed of the scene."

"Good. That beats the hell out of ESPN. Bring it up."

A lower ranking officer worked the controls frantically. The President wasn't known for being a patient man.

"Is it the Koreans? Did that maniac go over the line?"

The Admiral shook his head. "It's too soon to say."

The President took his seat, then pressed an intercom button. "Where's my omelette?" He turned his attention back to matters at hand. "For God's sake, Bill. What do we know?"

Not much, was what he wanted to say. But the President was not a suitable audience for that kind of ambiguity. "It appears the attack originated from a sea based weapon. The F-15, which was first on site, reported seeing something in the water. That was just before he disappeared from radar."

"A sub? I hate those things. Too damn sneaky, if you ask me. Say, what can those two-stage missiles do about a sub?"

The Admiral knew the President was fascinated with this new technology. It was a result of a research project designed to find conventional explosives that could mimic the damage of a nuclear weapon.

"If it's close enough to the surface, we can hit it with one hell of a shock wave."

"Good. I love the sounds of that. But what about those ships? Is there any kind of rescue under way?"

"We're moving every resource we have in the area. The problem is: Alaska is a big place. We've got forty-seven thousand miles of shoreline if you count all the inlets and islands. It's hard to cover when the primary response ship gets sunk."

"Forty-seven thousand miles. How is that possible? When did we let that happen?"

The Admiral didn't know how to respond.

"Well, that's one issue that won't be on the agenda any time soon. Oh, here we go."

The giant screen at the front of the room flickered to life.

"What are we looking at here? I can't make out a damn thing."

"Just a minute, Mr. President. Captain Telford, can you patch me through to those planes?"

"Yes sir. Your mike should give you direct access to their communications channel."

The Admiral pressed the key. "This is Admiral Bowles at the Command Center."

A tinny but clear voice responded. "This is Major Branton. I can hear you, Admiral."

"Good. Which of you is transmitting the video feed?"

"That would be me, sir."

"I'm here with the President. We'd like a better view. Can you bank your approach to get a better shot?"

"Yes sir. Stand by."

The picture moved and the ocean surface was soon visible. Other than a small amount of debris, there wasn't much visible.

"Is this the place?" the President asked. "Where is everything?"

"Is that the location, Major?"

"Yes sir."

The room grew quiet while they absorbed the implications.

The President was the first to speak. "How long until rescue teams arrive?"

Someone seated further back at the table responded. "The first choppers will be there in fifteen minutes, Mr. President."

"Okay, good. Now, how are we going to find who did this? What's the plan, Admiral?"

"There are four subs on the way. They are capable of sonar and audio tracking. We'll find them, whoever they are."

"Make sure you do. And try to keep this quiet. The damn media will lose their minds when they hear about this."

"I can manage that at our end, sir. But thousands of people with phones on the cruise ship…no doubt this has already leaked."

The President stood. "Bill, this is a non-negotiable situation. Find the bastards and blow them out of the water."

"Yes, Mr. President."

"Keep me posted. I've got some trade talks to salvage and an omelette to eat."

"Yes sir."

"Oh, and Bill?"

"Sir?"

"Have those Raptors check out the coastline. Also, any other resources you need are yours, understand?"

"Yes sir. Thank you Mr. President."

They all stood as the Commander-in-Chief stalked out.

It was hours later when the President summoned the Admiral to the Oval Office. The Admiral looked uncharacteristically ruffled.

"Bill, what the hell? I was expecting to hear something before now."

"We're smothering the area with subs and AWACS, sir. We also have the satellites sweeping the coastal regions."

"And…"

"So far, nothing."

"Damn it, Bill! That's unacceptable. All that technology and we can't find one sub?"

"I know, sir. I feel the same way."

"It's not some new, undetectable kind of war machine, is it? Like in that Tom Clancy movie?"

"At this point, Mr. President, I honestly don't know how to answer that."

The President blew a stream of air between pursed lips. "What about Russia? Remember Putin saying they have the best prostitutes? Maybe he has VD and it's affecting his mind. That would explain a lot."

"Sir, we have another sub on the way. The sonar man on it is our very best. They say he can hear a whale pass gas from twenty miles away."

"Twenty miles, you say? Well, that's a helpful skill. Get him there, Bill. I want closure on this business and I want it today. CNN is going roast me on this, trust me. I need answers before that happens."

A man in full military uniform stepped into the room. "Admiral?"

"What is it, Major?"

"Sir, I have the latest update from the scene."

The President responded first. "Let's have it, then."

"Rescuers have pulled eight people from the water still alive. One of them is the pilot of the F-15 that crashed."

The President slapped the top of his desk. Both men jumped. "Outstanding! Can we talk to him? Maybe he can give some focus to this whole escapade."

"What kind of condition are they in?" the Admiral asked.

"Shock and hypothermia are the predominant issues, sir."

"What are the odds of survival?"

"I don't know, Admiral. Rescue personnel were "cautiously optimistic" at last report."

The President walked over, standing uncomfortably close to the Admiral. "This is a matter of national security, Admiral. I want somebody to talk to that pilot at the very least—the other survivors too, if at all possible. Somebody must have seen something that will help us to sort this out. And by sort this out, I mean blow the bastards responsible straight to hell."

The Admiral nodded. "I'll make the arrangements, Mr. President."

"Good. Keep me appraised, Bill. Wake me up if you have to."

"Yes sir. Major, come with me." They both marched towards the door.

The President wandered over to the window, staring out over the expansive lawn. "God help you when we find you, whoever you are. You picked the wrong country to mess with."

The monster had fed well, but left before cleaning up every possible meal source. Two attacks hadn't caused serious injury, but the reality that this spot was becoming increasingly hostile, coupled with the temporary cessation of its hunger pangs, gave it the notion that it should leave. Submerged, it swam southward along the coast, its powerful tail moving it at a rapid clip.

Its alien metabolism, engineered for fast growth spurts whenever possible, was in overdrive. The energy provided by the huge repast would be converted to the nutritional elements that would convert to body mass, adding to its bulk. This sudden increase in size sometimes resulted in pain for the monster as its body changed, but it was a desire bred into it. Only one thought motivated its actions, even now, pain or not.

It needed to find its next meal.

7

It was the most secure meeting possible. Three people sat around the Oval Office desk. Doors were closed and the Secret Service was authorized to keep everyone out, using force if necessary.

"Three villages in Alaska, you say?" The President frowned. It had been two days since the attacks along the coast and nothing had been resolved. Russia had denied any responsibility in the strongest possible terms, even volunteering its entire fleet to aid in the search for the guilty party. That wasn't a guarantee, but the truth was, it didn't make sense for the Russians to pull a stunt like this. Too much to lose, with little to gain.

"That's right, Mr. President." Tom Collier was the man in charge of the CIA's ultra-secret security division. Very few people knew it even existed. He oversaw a broad-based grouping of military and security departments.

"Tell me again how you think this could be connected."

He shrugged. "It's a weak premise, I'll grant you that. But we are desperate for connections at this point, correct?"

The President scowled. "You could say that."

The other person at the table, Secretary of State Kowalski, turned her icy blue eyes on Collier. "Stop farting around, Tom. Time is of the essence."

"Whatever destroyed these villages had the ability to blow up the structures. There was no evidence of an actual bomb or missile. Nonetheless, the homes exploded. Whatever did this damage could also have the ability to damage ships and planes. Theoretically."

The President's face was growing redder. "This is all so much gibberish, Tom. What the hell does it even mean? You have no idea what did this? How is that possible?"

"No survivors, ergo no witnesses."

Kowalski stared hard at the CIA boss, her eyes boring into Collier's. White House staff knew she had the uncanny ability to read people and deduce what was going on in their minds. She was a deadly poker player. The President was aware that she had this skill, which was why he wanted her to sit in on this meeting. "You know."

He raised his eye brows. "I beg your pardon?"

"I can read you," she said. "You know."

"For God's sake, Collier!" The President was furious. "Tell me everything now, or you'll be looking for another job before you leave this room."

Despite the pressure being applied, Collier still hesitated before responding. "Very well, Mr. President. Be forewarned that this info is disturbing."

"Spill it, man."

He cleared his throat, collecting his thoughts. "Very well. First of all, regarding the village attacks, it isn't true that there were no survivors. A young child did survive the first one, but we've kept that knowledge under wraps for the protection of the boy. He couldn't tell us much, but he did see what was responsible."

"Well, what was it?"

"In his words, a monster."

The President leaned back. "Come on, Tom. Everything from a cow to a delivery truck looks like a monster to a kid. This tells us nothing."

"After we interviewed him, we were able to somewhat confirm what he told us from physical evidence on the ground, and satellite imagery."

"You have a picture of it? Why the hell didn't you say so in the first place?"

"It's not very detailed. And…it didn't come from one of ours."

"Where'd it come from, then?"

"A Russian spy satellite."

The President looked surprised. "How did you talk them into sharing that?"

"We didn't."

"Then how did you get it?"

Collier hesitated long enough for the President to figure it out.

"Oh. I suppose I'm not supposed to ask how that's possible."

"I'd rather you didn't," Collier said.

"Fine. Forget all that. What the hell was it? Did you bring the images with you?"

Collier squirmed just a little. "No. They weren't very detailed anyway."

"Then why did you bring this up in the first place? Besides, I'd rather be the judge of that. I'm the President and I want to see them."

"I can bring them up on my phone, if you insist."

"Oh sure. A poorly detailed image on a three inch screen. Don't do me any favors, Tom. By the way, how do you feel about flipping burgers for a career move?"

"I can…have them brought here. It will only take a few minutes."

"Time sensitive, Tom. Does that mean anything to you?"

The Secretary of State shook her head. "You're so full of shit, Collier. No wonder you got this job."

"The hell with it," the President said. "Bring them up and give me your damn phone. No more screwing around. I'm not some lackey or idiot reporter. I'm the Commander-in-Chief. No more evasiveness, Collier. Lay it all out, nice and clear. The next time I discover you held back any kind of information, I'm going to instruct our fine Secretary of State here to kick you right in the balls. And check out those shoes if you think that idea sounds like fun."

Her expression suggested that she might consider doing it.

"Here you go, sir." He extended his phone.

The President laid his glasses on the table, held the phone close, squinting. "You weren't kidding about one thing. This image is useless. All I can see is a blur."

"You can zoom in, Mr. President. Just use your fingers. It does help."

"I'm going to use my fingers to choke you, Collier. Why didn't you do that before you handed it to me? I thought you were supposed to be so smart. You're coming across as a dufus right now." He adjusted the screen. "My God. There it is. But what is it? It's a big, black blob. What have you learned from this?"

Collier struggled to maintain his poise. "It's not mechanical, sir."

"Not mechanical? What does that mean?"

"It's alive."

The president paused. "Alive? Seriously? And it's blowing up villages and sinking our ships?"

"That's what I believe sir, yes."

"How's that possible? I mean, what the hell is it? From this, it looks like a pregnant rhinoceros."

"We don't know, Mr. President."

"Then find out! Do I have to do all the thinking for you? What the hell do you do all day—sit at your desk staring off into space?"

"We have some limited evidence from the village sites but it doesn't tell us much. The navy is trying to track it now. We suspect that it is following the coast southward."

"How far southward?"

"We don't know."

"Well, if you're right and it goes far enough, it will be in Canadian waters. What the hell are they going to do…throw beavers at it?"

The room grew silent.

"Should I call the Prime Minister and give him a heads-up? Their navy must have some canoes or kayaks, or something they can put in the water."

More silence ensued.

"All right," the President said. "Get back to your department, Collier, and figure this out. You contact me immediately if you find this thing or come up with some useful information—you understand?"

"Yes Mr. President," he replied as he stood, thankful to be dismissed. He wasted no time exiting the room.

"My God," the President exclaimed. "I would never accuse him of being proficient at his job."

The Secretary of State remained silent. The President knew it wasn't due to a lack of interest on her part. Only he got to throw insults around randomly at high officials.

"What do you make of this, Kowalski? Seems like something out of a James Cameron film."

Many of the President's observations filtered through his knowledge of modern culture. Too many, she sometimes thought. "I don't know. You don't think Collier made this up as a smokescreen to hide the fact that they haven't found any real evidence yet?"

"Naw. Too bizarre, even for Collier's department. There's something to this. Say, you don't think the Commies came up with some new biological weapon, do you? All they have to do is turn it loose and deny responsibility. It's not likely they tattooed a hammer and sickle on it to establish ownership."

The Secretary shook her head. "I think we need more info before making assumptions."

The President nodded. "You're right. I wish I had more confidence that it was coming. Well, I'm going to call the Canadians and see what they have to say. Don't they have their own version of the Loch Ness monster up there? They call it Hokie-Pokie or something like that. Maybe that's what this is."

"I'll give you some privacy, sir."

"Thanks for sitting in. I love it when you make Collier squirm."

"My pleasure, Mr. President."

The monster attacked and sank a fishing boat during the night, but found that it didn't provide much in the way of food. It needed better sources.

At daybreak, it came ashore, doing some recognizance. It found rugged landscape that was inhabited only by small birds and animals, with an occasional moose thrown in for good measure. These creatures had camouflage and instincts to help them avoid contact with danger. They were also spread thin enough that a feast was not possible. The monster went back into the water, utilizing an inherent ability to sense direction, then continued swimming southward along the coast. Sooner or later, something more substantial would turn up.

8

"Watch your head!"

Dan Landers bent down, lowering his upper body to accommodate the movement of the boom as it swung past. Sailing was nice, but involved too much work for him. He preferred to start the motor and drive the boat like a car. As they moved along in silence, there was no doubt it was a wonderful way to enjoy what had to be one of the most beautiful places on earth—Vancouver harbor. Besides that, his future son-in-law was the one doing all the work. He held up his phone, snapping a shot of the high rise buildings along the shore.

"Take some with the bridge in the background," his wife Cathy directed.

A pontoon plane was taking off in the distance, commanding his attention. He swivelled to keep it centered in the photo.

"Hey, don't fall overboard." His future son-in-law, Chuck, had his best interests in mind, but Dan was too independent to accept such banal advice.

"You just steer the boat and keep your hands off my daughter."

"Dad!" Chelsea, his daughter looked horrified. She glared at him over the top of her dark sunglasses to ensure he could see her eyes.

His wife shook her head. "You'll have to ignore him, just like I do."

Dan was impervious to her insults at this point in their relationship. He concentrated on taking pictures. He turned towards the bridge, zooming in.

A few moments later, he shielded the screen against the glare of the sun with his hand while reviewing the most recent shots. They were good, he decided. He would send them to his co-workers back home to annoy them with how much fun he was having while they were still slaving away. The thought of it put a smile on his face.

"Dan?"

"What honey?" He continued his review.

"What is that?"

He looked up. "What is what?"

Cathy pointed. "Over there."

He swivelled in the right direction. He saw nothing noteworthy.

"It's in the water," she elaborated.

He saw it now. Or at least he saw something. There was a large dark patch in the otherwise blue surface. "That's weird. Hey, hotshot, what am I looking at?"

Chuck followed the direction his future father-in-law was staring. "I don't know. Never seen anything like it before."

They were sailing in a direction that would keep them well clear. No adjustments at the helm were made. Dan set his phone to resume taking photos, trying to get the dark shape in the centre of the screen.

"Dad…" This time it was Chelsea adding her input.

He kept his eyes on the phone. "What sweetheart?"

"I think it's coming up."

He started snapping pictures. "You're right. Thanks for the warning." He prepared to take some action shots. Maybe he could catch a sub as it emerged. How cool would that be?

"Umm, dad…"

The water bulged and the dark shape broke the surface. It rose up until there was no doubt about two things, as far as Dan was concerned. It was huge, and unlike anything he had ever seen in his life.

"Holy crap!" He put down the phone after snapping a couple more pics. This thing was no sub. It looked to be alive. He thought of the Saturday afternoon monster matinees that he watched when he was a kid. But they were make-believe. He then came up with another reason why he preferred motorized boats.

Speed.

The monster took a moment to get comfortable with this new environment. It scanned with all its abilities, making decisions.

There was a proliferation of boats in the water, but most were small, and none seemed to have a large number of creatures aboard. The monster didn't want a snack—it needed to feast. Fish had sustained it during the years of slow growth while living in Illiamna Lake. It instinctively knew that significant food sources were now required to reach the next stage in its development. Thus far, the creatures that had colonized in these artificial environments had proved to be the only suitable alternative. It turned its attention to the towering edifices clustered on the land surrounding the bay. It swam closer and was rewarded. There were a large number of creatures along the shore. The buildings were also full of life, based on infra-red scans.

This could be good.

Paulie Esposito had been running the overhead crane since he was nothing more than a kid. He couldn't begin to guess the gross tonnage he had unloaded during his career, but it was a lot. Nowadays, his thoughts turned frequently to packing it in—retiring and moving somewhere south. But not while operating the crane; that required his full and constant attention. The two-way radio crackled to life. Paulie released his grip on the crane controls. He wasn't lifting anything unless the act was the sole focus of his attention.

"Holy shit, Paulie! Do you see that?"

The question was nonsense without some sort of context. Buddy and co-worker, Brad, wasn't always the most coherent communicator. Paulie grabbed the dangling mike, keying it. "What do you mean? See what?"

"Just look at the water!"

Paulie couldn't imagine directions that vague would help narrow his search enough to guarantee results. Vancouver Harbor was enormous. But when he turned to his right, shifting his focus, the reason for all the excitement was clear.

"What *is* that?" Paulie squinted to sharpen his long-distance focus. A dark abomination the size of his apartment building was moving inwards, plowing through the otherwise scenic blue water. His mind had no way to process the appearance of this horrible creature. His initial reaction was concern, transitioning to fear. He was sitting in a small control room over one hundred feet off the ground, mounted atop a metal framework whose structural integrity he had never doubted—until now. He keyed the mike again, this time more frantically.

"Brad, get down! That thing's coming straight for us."

Paulie dropped the mike, content to let it dangle, and reached to open the door. He could only go so fast when climbing. He didn't want to waste another second.

The monster stopped its approach, doing another diagnostic. There was a proliferation of both living things and mechanical devices stretched across the shore. Beyond that, an endless multitude of structures stretching high above the ground, full of food sources according to its scanning results. But the attacks suffered at the cruise ship feast caused it to adopt a more cautious approach. Rather than rushing out of the water, it stabilized, taking aim for a preliminary attack. The plates along its side began to pivot. Air pressure began to build. Given the size it had grown to, this blast would be significantly stronger than the ones previously unleashed. The proboscis tuned to fire a broad stream, and the pressure discharged.

A deep, thunderous boom, like the blast from an enormous, demonic horn sounded as the wave of destruction flew across the harbor, rippling the surface of the otherwise calm waters as it honed in on its target. It struck with terrible results. Small boats capsized while huge cargo ships rocked violently. Metal twisted, tearing loose from its seams and glass panes shattered. Human bodies were thrown through the air, until they crashed into something that stopped their momentum. Ears drums burst, noses bled through damaged sinuses and skulls cracked from the violent vibrations.

Paulie, going hand over hand down the ladder as fast as he could, passed out when the wave hit him and commenced bouncing from one rung to another until gravity was satisfied.

The monster was pleased with the results, deciding to fire off a second attack. Then the feasting would begin.

9

Rousting the President from his sleep was a dangerous venture at best. During the moments of transition before waking, he tended to snap at anything and anyone in his path. Preliminary grousing now complete, POTUS walked down the hall with purpose. Wrapped in a robe that gaped in a most unwelcome manner, his pre-routine hair would have been laughable on anyone else. But his scowl foretold of the reaction any comments on his appearance would bring. It was out of the question.

Admiral Bowles appeared out of a side door, falling into step beside the Commander-in-Chief.

"Well? Why am I up at this ungodly hour, Bill? Do you have good news of some sort?"

The Admiral sighed. "I'm afraid not, Mr. President. We believe the thing responsible for the Alaska incident is attacking the Vancouver area as we speak."

"You believe it is attacking or you believe it's the same monster?"

"We *know* it's attacking, sir. We *believe* it's the same creature."

"Let's hope there's only one violent monster terrorizing the west coast. I think we can go on that assumption until proven otherwise. What are the Canadians doing about it besides screaming in fear?"

"They had a destroyer at anchor in the harbor, but the creature, whatever it is, has moved inland, out of range."

"Inland, you say?"

"Yes, sir. It has damaged a number of buildings in downtown Vancouver."

"Good lord! It's just like Godzilla. What's the contingency plan?"

"For who, sir?"

"Let's start with the Canadians."

"They are moving troops into the area, but they won't be ready to engage until deployment is finished, sometime tomorrow morning. Keep in mind we're ahead of them by several hours—the sun is just starting to set on the west coast. They also have several CF-18's available from a base in Alberta, but if they attack it, they'll do more damage to the city."

The President scowled. "So they're not doing anything. Big surprise there. The Prime Minister is probably thinking about apologizing to it. You'd imagine with all the hockey sticks floating around up there, they could at least slash away at it. What about us? What are we doing?"

"That's why you're up, Mr. President. We need your authorization to set up our response. Keep in mind, sir, Seattle is very close to this area and accessible by water."

"The hell with that, Admiral. You're about to get authorization to use everything we have in our arsenal. We're going to put an end to this nonsense, and right quick."

"Yes, sir." One thing about the President, he was never indecisive or reluctant when it came to matters of national security. The Admiral felt that it overcame many of his other flaws.

Rosita Moraliz had been cleaning the same set of offices for eight years now. It meant being on the afternoon shift, but at least it was steady work. And there was nobody around to interfere with what she was doing. She put on her headphones tuning out everything else. Thus equipped, her shift should fly past.

When the hydro went out, her first thought was to call her husband, but the phone lines were also down. She resorted to using her cell with the cheap, reduced minutes plan, but it too was unable to complete a call. So she wandered over to the window, enjoying the view of downtown Vancouver from seven stories above the ground, waiting for the power to come back on.

"Oye!" From her vantage point, it seemed that all the lights in Vancouver were out. That wasn't good. This could be a late night for her. She wasn't allowed to leave until her work was completed. Looking out into the gloom, she thought she could perceive some movement on the street below. Optimistic that it could be a work crew, she tried to improve her focus. That turned out to be a mistake.

"¡Me cago en la mar!" She took a step back, covering her gaping mouth with her hand. In the darkness, a shape took form. It was horrifying beyond her worst nightmares. An enormous, lumbering monster that had no business existing in this world was ramming itself along the street, crushing cars and toppling poles. The mystery behind the power outage was now solved. Even from her elevation, the massive creature's back would be above her level as it trundled past her building.

The monster used its attack once again. A deep, reverberating sound from an otherworldly instrument filled the air as a pressure wave flew past. Rosita's entire body vibrated. An acute, sudden-onset headache tried to split her skull open. Windows, including the one in front of her, shattered into pieces, falling to the street below in a tinkling cacophony of destruction. She screamed, stepping back to avoid the gravitational pull that existed only in her terrified imagination. That was when she heard a sound never produced before in this world. The monster, now huge and imposing, celebrated its success in finding easy meals by letting loose a deafening roar.

This new sound resembled fingernails being raked across a chalkboard, played back through a concert-sized sound system, while ghouls from the abyss shrieked discordant background lyrics in support. Rosita and countless other poor souls added their own screams to the chorus. It was an appropriate accompaniment to the end of life as they knew it.

The monster continued feeding.

Aya walked into the office, surprised to see what amounted to the entire day staff, six people in all, crowded around the wall-mounted television screen.

"What's going on?" He could see the CNN logo, but the image itself was dark and blurry.

"Vancouver is under attack!" their dispatcher Anne exclaimed, leaving Aya to wonder who was taking incoming calls.

"Attack by whom?" If he was forced to guess, he would have gone with Asian street gangs. Even with his best efforts, the picture was still too chaotic to discern.

"A monster," she said, dropping her voice to a whisper, as if that would somehow help the situation.

The headline scrolled across the bottom, announcing the very thing she had just repeated.

"The entire downtown area is destroyed," she said, as she tore herself away, moving back towards her station.

Aya sidled up to his superior. "What's your take on this, Bill?"

The Sergeant's gaze never wavered. "Beats the hell out of me. Witnesses claim there's a gigantic monster destroying buildings."

"Really?" Even with the news coverage as confirmation, Aya was doubtful. The networks hadn't won any awards for accurate and impartial reporting recently.

"Yeah." The Sergeant turned to look at his best officer. "Almost sounds familiar, doesn't it?"

"What do you mean?"

"That doesn't remind you of anything that happened around here lately?"

Aya was thunderstruck. That thought hadn't occurred to him. "You think there's a connection to Malhulik?"

"I don't know."

The group continued watching.

"All right, everybody," Sergeant Taft said. "We've got a job to do. Let's try to tear ourselves away from this noise box."

Everyone began to move away. Aya followed the Sergeant into his office.

"Don't tell me you've got a screw loose over this thing," his boss admonished. "There's nothing I can tell you, Aya. I know the same things you know."

Aya collected his thoughts. "If it's the Malhulik monster, then our file on the case becomes a little more important, wouldn't you say?"

"What file?" Taft said. "The FBI took over the case, remember? If there's a connection, then they'll be the ones to make it."

Aya remained calm and stoic. "I suppose you're right."

The Sergeant was settling in at his desk. "Of course I am. I know it's human nature when something big happens to find a way to make a connection or get involved in some way, but this is as far out of our jurisdiction as you can get. Besides, I need you to assist with the prostitution sting today, remember?"

"I remember."

"Good. You can swing by when you're finished to get an update if you want."

"You want me to check in?" It sounded more official to paint it in that way.

"Yeah. Check in."

Aya nodded, turning to go.

The two CF-18 Super Hornets flew in tight formation over what remained of Vancouver. The rising sun revealed the full effects of the attack. Both pilots dealt with their shock while trying to remain focused and professional. They were finding it to be a struggle.

"Bank left." Major Terry Melnik was in control of the pair and was doing a masterful job of keeping his voice clipped and steady.

The trail of destruction originated by the water front, meandered through downtown, and led back to the harbor. There were no signs of whatever was responsible and that pissed the pilots off as much as anything. They wanted to shoot something in retribution for their devastated countrymen. So far, no opportunity presented itself.

"No signs of the target, control. Looks like it has gone back to the water, over."

"Roger. Do a sweep of the harbor and off-shore area."

"Roger that."

They passed over the warehouse district. What they saw both shocked and saddened them—more devastation on land, continuing into the water. Remains of ships both large and small were strewn about. Several fires blazed away on land and sea.

"Viper Two."

Melnik was surprised by the call. His partner had been silent throughout the entire mission up until now. "Go ahead, Viper Two."

"I have eyes on something in the water. Three o'clock, maybe two clicks out. It's a large, dark spot. Looks like something just under the surface of the water."

Melnik, with his pilot's vision, had no problem picking it out. "Roger, Viper Two. Bank right. We're coming around."

Even at a reduced cruising speed, the jets ate up the distance fast.

"Let's dip the wing for a better view." Melnik banked his plane, taking a good look. Adrenalin began to kick in. He was both excited and abhorred by what he saw.

"Control, Viper One. We have eyes on something big in the water. It is not, I repeat, not a ship. I believe it is our target. Request permission to go weapons hot and engage."

"Viper One, do you have a clear shot, over?"

"Control, target is submerged. It is still visible, though. We might be able to bring it up."

"Viper One, be advised that this thing might have the ability to damage your plane, over."

Fuck that, Melnik thought. *Not if I damage it first.* "Roger Control. We have clear sight for a shot. This is a first strike opportunity, over."

"What about collateral damage to the harbor, Viper One?"

How to answer that, Melnik thought. "Control, there's not much left to worry about. The harbor is devastated."

There was a short but painful delay before the next response came.

"Roger that. Viper One, you are cleared to engage, over."

Now the floodgate was open and adrenalin came in a rushing torrent. Melnik fought to keep his hands steady. "Roger that, Control." He turned his attention to his partner flying a short distance away.

"Weapons hot, Viper Two. Break on my mark."

"Roger that."

Melnik was pleased with the icy cold tone of the voice. "First run is Sparrows, Viper One. Three, two, one, break."

The two sleek aircraft turned in opposite directions, spreading apart to achieve a better defensive position. In a worst-case scenario, this thing would only be able to attack one of them. As they continued along the arcing course, their jets began to converge.

"Fox One!" Melnik unleashed his terrible weapon, breaking sharply away.

"Fox One!" His partner followed suit, breaking in the opposite direction.

"Weapons away!" Melnik yelled into his radio while turning to watch their smoke trails as they approached the target at supersonic speed.

The monster's senses were developing as it grew. That, coupled with the fact that it had been attacked by a jet fighter before, made it more wary. When the two CF-18's thundered past on their first sweep, the vibration of the noise alerted the monster to their presence. Powerful but not foolish, it dove for the bottom of the harbor.

The first missile struck the water, exploding on impact. An impressive plume of water was thrown skyward. The second struck beside it with the same results.

"Viper Two, get back into formation. We'll do a pass to see what we accomplished."

They regrouped, executing a slow turn. Melnik would be more careful this time. If this thing was capable of defending itself, two missile strikes might convince it to go on the offensive.

"Stay sharp. We'll go overhead and have a good look."

"Roger that, Viper One."

As they approached, initial signs weren't promising. The dark patch had moved away. It seemed faded, an indication that it had gone deep.

"Control, Viper One. Target is still moving, over."

"Any signs of damage, Viper One?"

"Negative." Melnik was cursing under his breath. The Sparrow was the most powerful weapon they carried. If that hadn't worked, they could do no more than watch this thing slink away.

"Viper One, do we re-engage?"

Melnik had never wanted to say yes more in his life, but reality dictated that it would be a wasted effort. "Negative, Viper Two. Let's slow down and conserve fuel. We'll track it as far as we can. Control, do we have any naval assets in the area?"

"Negative, Viper One. We had a destroyer in the harbor, but it was damaged in the attack."

"Roger, Control. We're going to track it as far as we can. If it resurfaces, we will re-engage."

"Roger that."

Following it wasn't going to be as satisfying as shooting the damn thing, Melnik thought as he tucked in behind it, but they still had a job to do.

"Standard formation, Viper Two. Try not to let it get out of sight." The problem was that once it got out of the harbor, the water dropped off quickly. The monster could take a dive and disappear. They could only speculate on where it would go or what it would do next.

10

The White House Situation Room was a very busy place. The President glared at the people surrounding the huge table.

"Okay. Let's start with our state of readiness. Please tell me that if that monster attacks Seattle we won't be caught with our fly open with and an embarrassed look on our face."

Admiral Bowles stood to address the Commander-in-Chief.

"We have an excellent security perimeter in place, Mr. President. We have a coordinated blanket of both naval, air and land based assets in position, and ready for immediate engagement should it become necessary."

"Be specific, Bill. Generalities are useless and bore the hell out of me."

"Yes sir. As we aren't sure what we're dealing with here, we thought it prudent to take a very broad-based approach. Our automated missile security defense system is in place and scanning as we speak. We have elements of the 4th armoured division holding position along the shore with all of our latest technologies incorporated."

"Does that mean you have those new auto-fire guns there?"

The Admiral knew not to show any uncertainty in front of his boss. "No, Mr. President. They are only effective if we know where the attack will occur, or if we're defending a very narrow, specific area."

"That sounds exceptionally useful. Maybe if we had enough of them, we could cover wider areas. Did that ever occur to anybody?"

"That matter is in the hands of the appropriation committee, Mr. President."

"Perfect. I'm overdue to show up and start yelling at them anyway. I'll put that on my agenda. What else?"

"We have AWAKS and attack aircraft in the air patrolling 24/7."

"Do they have those two stage bombs?"

"Yes, Mr. President. And we have B-2's with specials available should we have an offshore attack possibility present itself."

"Hold on, Admiral. You know authorization has to go through me. That kind of talk even makes me nervous."

"We are well aware, Mr. President. We're just covering all bases."

"Fine. What about the navy?"

"Yes sir. We have the entire 3rd Fleet deployed, with certain assets from the 4th fleet on the way. We also have the new stealth cruiser off shore. She's a fine piece of equipment."

"All right. Good." The President looked around the room making people squirm in their seats. "You know what I miss? Battleships. There's something about firing those 16 inch guns that makes you want to drop a load in your pants—if you know what I'm saying."

Nobody replied.

"What about the Canadians? Were they able to smack it with a paddle or something?"

The Admiral cleared his throat. "They engaged it with CF-18's. They were unable to inflict serious damage."

"Canadian fighters, huh. What do they fire from those things— chunks of frozen moose meat?"

"No sir. They used Sparrows...the exact same weapon system we sometimes utilize."

"All right, no need to be defensive on their behalf. We're all friends. Anyway, there aren't any Canadians in the room. Are there?"

Another uncomfortable silence fell over the room.

"Fine. Admiral, lock this down. Keep a finger on the trigger. The instant thing shows its ugly face, blow it into a billion tiny pieces. Is that clear enough?"

"Yes, Mr. President. We'll be ready."

"Good. Let me know as soon as anything happens. I'm sure you can find another meal or some other small pleasure to interrupt. But I can live with that. Focus on this, everyone—when you get the shot, take it. Don't stop to think about it or wonder if you need permission. I'm giving that authority to you right now. And one other thing—don't miss." With this final admonition, he stalked out of the room.

The monster had powerful senses and an intelligence that suited its purpose well. But it was not omnipotent. After the attack from the CF-18's, it moved away from shore into deep waters. Neither the cold, nor the dark, nor the increased pressure bothered it in any way. Now it felt secure.

This new course took it away from Seattle, leaving that fine city safe and untouched. It continued a steady, strong swim southward. The monster didn't know what the State of California was, but now set a course that would facilitate contact. The San Andreas Fault was no longer the most imminent threat to the coast.

Aya wondered why he was here (and not for the first time). He sat cross-legged, wearing deer skin shorts and nothing else. Inside the sweat lodge, no other clothing would be tolerable. The chief had been insistent that Aya attend. So here he was, his skin soaked already.

A fire burned in the center of the lodge, dug into a shallow hole. The shelter was not much more than a large tent, animal skins stretched over supple green branches. But it, and the ceremony it housed, held great meaning to his people. Indeed, there was a sense of foreboding in the atmosphere, as well as the smoke.

Only those with experience and knowledge of the ceremony were allowed to conduct one. The chief of the local tribe sat across from Aya, cross-legged, deep in meditation. His thick, grey hair showed no signs of sweat. The expression on his face was serene, his body language was that of a person comfortable in their environment. That left Aya staring into space, waiting impatiently for the whole process to end.

"Does the ceremony bother you?"

Aya frowned without realizing it. "No, of course not."

The chief opened his eyes. "Good. Because this is and always has been the way of our people."

Aya, not for the first time, was aware of how much he had adapted to the modern world. It was pulling him away. "I know."

"But there is more that you don't."

What did that mean? Aya was hoping this wouldn't turn into a lecture. "It's hard to find time for the old ways. I have a life in the city to attend to."

"Old? Is that how you think of them?" The chief's voice had a gruff tone of authority.

"You know what I mean." Aya found himself getting uncomfortable. How could the chief sit for hours like that?

"You have been chosen." The chief laid it out bare, offering no further explanation. The words hung in the air.

Aya felt a flicker of panic. He hoped the chief didn't want him to take over some job here on the reservation, using his heritage as leverage to guilt him into accepting it. There wasn't time to take on anything else. Either way, the question had to be asked. "Chosen for what?"

"The real question is—chosen by whom?"

"Let me guess. The tribal leaders?"

"No. They know nothing of this matter."

"What matter?"

"There are voices crying out to you. Have you not heard them?"

Why plural, Aya wondered. "Voices?"

The chief settled back in, reclosing his eyes. "I hear them even now. They cry out in terror. They cry for help. They look with desperation for an answer. But only one can bring it. That one is you."

Aya was lost. Backed into a corner, he saw no way out. Truth was his lone remaining avenue. "I don't understand your words. I hear nothing."

"You don't hear, but can you feel?"

This wasn't helping. Aya wanted out. His mind drifted away to a trivial distraction—a coffee and donut while reading the daily paper back in the city.

"Do you feel nothing?" The chief's voice rose in volume until he was almost yelling.

Aya shrugged. He was sorry to have pissed off the old man. "I feel like there is weight in the air. It feels oppressive."

This seemed to appease him. "Yes. Then you are on the correct path. But you must go further. Close your eyes. Follow me. Forget the distractions that swirl in your mind. Come back to the ways of your ancestors. Allow the spirits to lead you."

Disappointed, Aya knew he had just been sentenced to more time squatting in the dirt. He waited for further instruction or admonition, but the chief was silent.

Now what, he thought. He closed his eyes, seeking diversion, but there was none. Even the sounds from outside were muffled and a perfect silence filled the air. The soft crackle of the fire was the only audible input for his straining ears.

Great. This was going to be fun. Aya thought of a snippet from a Gordon Lightfoot song which spoke of minutes turning to hours. That was exactly what was happening. He was trapped here.

The oppressive atmosphere wrapped itself around him like a blanket. There was nothing pleasant or comforting about it. It was brooding and foreboding, but the explanation of what it represented was cloaked, unreachable. There was something tangible there, but it remained hidden.

Show yourself, Aya thought. *Let's get this over with.* He felt like his request had moved him closer to the source. He was now on a more perilous portion of the path. Darkness so deep that it was palpable moved towards him. Even though Aya knew he was safe in the hut, a fear started to take hold of his emotions.

Now he heard wind, distant but strong. It moaned and howled like a living thing. It was coming from the darkness. And it was getting closer.

Aya tried to open his eyes and found he could not. He then found something equally disconcerting. He could now hear the voices.

They weren't speaking to him at all. They were screaming. The darkness overtook them and they succumbed to a fear so strong and pervasive, it was irrational. There wasn't even a thread of sanity in the piercing shrieks flashing through Aya's mind, making him wince. It was mindless terror. Like an element from the periodic table, the chaos and horror was basic, pure and undiluted. The voices went to their doom knowing full well how awful the process would be. And it stole away the very substance of their being.

The vision grew darker. A form began to take shape. It was so foreign that Aya could make no sense of it as it approached. As it came into focus, Aya felt an all-encompassing foreboding unlike anything he had ever experienced before. There was one thing he did perceive and it was overwhelming.

Whatever this was, it meant to do great harm.

A blunt face, with alien features and malice so strong it took Aya's breath away, appeared from the depths of blackness. He felt an urgent need to move away, but his body would not respond. A gaping maw like a living doorway to eternal damnation opened and panic set in as neared. Aya couldn't scream, but twisted and moaned as he awaited the end.

The beast roared.

The sound was a twisted abomination of noise—metal tearing, damaged whistles shrieking, unworldly creatures howling. It was so loud. It drowned out everything else in a show of complete domination. Aya, still immobile, waited for his eardrums to burst or his head to split, whichever happened first.

But neither did, and the cry of pristine evil at last ceased, allowing him to release the breath he hadn't known he was holding. Seemingly satisfied, it turned, disappearing back into the darkness. Aya watched the dark creature go, noticing the heavy plating on its sides. Somehow he sensed they were impenetrable and made the beast invulnerable. His heart filled with absolute sorrow. Why had he been called to see this? There was nothing he, or anyone else for that matter, could do to thwart this darkness. Absolute hopelessness and utter despair gripped his soul.

The creature stopped. Aya feared it would turn back towards him. Instead, it seemed to be preparing itself for another attack. That was when Aya saw it. The plates, those indestructible shields, opened. It wasn't by much, nor was it for long. But inside, behind the plates, was vulnerability.

Aya clung to the slim hope offered by this revelation. Light began to filter in as he shed a single tear of anguish.

He opened his eyes, squinting at the light, even in the gloom of the hut. The chief no longer sat across from him.

He stood, collecting his thoughts. He made his way to the door, lifting the flap and stooping to fit through the opening.

"There you are." The chief walked towards him, as if he had known the exact moment that Aya was going to exit the hut.

"Thanks for leaving me the moment you finished your pep talk," Aya said.

The chief smiled. "You talk nonsense. You've been in there by yourself for the past two hours."

His words hit Aya like a truck. Could that be possible? It had seemed more like two minutes. "Are you serious?"

The chief nodded. He now wore a fringed deerskin jacket; effects of the sweat long since dissipated. "Did you hear the voices?"

"Yes."

"What did they tell you?" The chief seemed to know all the answers except that one.

"They didn't tell me anything. I need to get dressed."

The chief frowned. "Nothing? Yet you heard them? They said nothing at all?"

Aya started towards his truck. The Sweat Lodge was the source of the vision and he wanted to get away from it. "They screamed. That's all. Over and over."

The chief stopped dead in his tracks. "Screamed?"

"That's right." Aya said, still walking. He reached his pickup, opening the door. His clothes were on the seat, but he could change later. Much later. After he had put some distance between himself and the reservation. "Thanks for the sweat. They say it's good for the skin."

The chief watched in silence as Aya started the truck, driving off.

11

The President was holding court while sitting behind his desk. As he was known to stalk about the Oval Office rather than being immobile, this was an unexpected deviation. Admiral Bowles wasn't sure which was preferable.

"Still nothing?"

"That's correct, Mr. President."

"We implement the largest military deployment on home soil since the civil war, and don't fire a single shot to justify it?"

"Not yet, sir."

"None of our attempts to track this thing, whatever it is, have been successful either?"

"That's also correct, sir."

"So where the hell is it?"

How do I respond to that, the Admiral wondered. "We don't have an answer, Mr. President."

"I already know that, Bill. For God's sake, I was being rhetorical. What I meant was, in the face of a complete lack of useful information, maybe it would be prudent to at least speculate. Where do you *think* it might be? Or has a single person in all our various branches of the military given that any thought?"

"Of course, Mr. President."

"Let me guess. The answer is that it's somewhere in the water."

The actual response was going to be more detailed and eloquent, but in the end, that was a decent summary of what he was going to say. The Admiral marvelled at how the President kept him off balance. "That's quite accurate, sir."

The President scowled. "So the remaining question is: what do we do now?"

The Admiral had given that a lot of thought. "I'd like to have some assets available further down the coast. At this point, we can't be certain that it won't still attack in the Seattle area, but the possibility that it is moving further south exists."

"What if it's moving north again?"

The Admiral nodded. "That is another possibility. But if you take Canada out of the equation, we don't have all that much to defend up there. All our major population centres are in the opposite direction."

"That's what we should focus on," the President said.

"Yes sir, I believe so."

The Commander-in-Chief nodded. "I agree. Can we cover a larger portion of the coast without spreading ourselves too thin, Bill?"

"Yes sir, we can. I already have a plan in place."

"Good. Then begin implementation immediately."

"Yes sir." The Admiral rose from his chair.

"Bill, one more thing."

"Yes sir?"

"Why are you looking at me funny? You've been doing it since you came in."

Off guard again, the Admiral thought. "Oh, it's just that you don't usually sit behind your desk for these meetings, sir. I suppose I was wondering why you were there."

"That's all? Talk about a lack of focus. Maybe I've got an intern under here, Bill. It's Oval Office tradition, you know? I'm trying to see things from the Democrat point of view."

The Admiral nodded, saying nothing. He didn't dare try to interpret the President's sense of humor.

"Get to work on that deployment, Admiral. Stop by later to brief me on how things are progressing."

"Yes sir." The Admiral walked out, thankful to do so.

Aya sat in the dark at the kitchen table with a small glass of milk in front of him, staring at the wall. He would have loved a coffee, but figured the caffeine would be counter-productive.

The harder he tried to force the vision out of his mind, the more entrenched it seemed to become. He had given up on sleeping some time ago, wandering out of bed. Now all he could think about was how tired he was going to be in the morning. It sucked reading someone their rights while stifling a yawn. Why did he go for that sweat? He should have known better. Whether you believed in that stuff or not, he knew it was not uncommon to be affected by it.

He pushed the chair away from the table, picked up his milk, and began walking around the room without purpose. The apartment wasn't huge. It didn't take long for the exercise to become tedious.

The monster reappeared in his imagination. Aya tried once again to remove it by force with no success. Left with frustrated wandering as the only available option, he returned to his pointless meanderings.

Then he heard something in his mind, a tiny, recognizable voice. *"The monster eated them up."*

"Denny." The boy from the village. The traumatized little urchin who didn't even want to talk about what he had seen back in Malhulik. Aya nodded in renewed understanding.

Maybe he wasn't the only one having visions of darkness.

The monster swam through the deep, chilling water. It had reached a size where its priorities had started to transform. Due to the power of its attacks, a new motivation was taking hold. Eating was still important, and to some extent always would be. But now it could set its sights on a loftier target.

This planet was now the monster's possession. It would live here for the duration of its life, utilizing the resources as it saw fit to sustain itself. That was its instinct—what it had been bred to do. This world would have to be subdued so that a safe, easy life could be enjoyed. Parthenogenesis, or asexual reproduction, would allow the monster to populate the planet with its own kind at some point in the future. First, there was still work to do.

The monster had been attacked. There was no doubt that these puny creatures had intended to do it harm, kill it if they could. They would have to be eliminated. Completely—along with anything else that posed a threat, real or perceived.

Its senses picked up a faint sound. A warbling cadence with a distinct pattern identified the source as something unnatural. The monster didn't know the meaning of the word *mechanical*, but it knew that sound meant that a grouping of these dangerous creatures was near. Civilization was lurking in that general direction.

The thought of it infuriated the monster. It changed course, heading in the direction of the noise. It was ready to establish itself as the alpha life form of this planet.

There was no doubt or hint of uncertainty in its focus. It would lay waste to this world in order to satisfy the growing anger inside it. This wasn't a foray to find the next snack.

This was war.

PFC Jayden Davis heard the soft thunder of a military plane flying at high altitude roll across San Francisco Bay. He looked across the water towards the Golden Gate Bridge, marvelling at the view. This deployment sure beat the hell out of being somewhere in the Middle East. The deep blue water was dotted with white sails from the yachting crowd, adding another element to the calendar page appearance of the world-class vista.

"Davis!"

Damn. Staff Sergeant Carl Withers didn't share his appreciation for the appearance of the scene.

"Yes, Staff Sergeant?"

"Is that Howitzer blocked and levelled?" The question was yelled, not spoken.

"Yes, Staff Sergeant."

"Are the shells placed and ready?"

"Not yet."

Withers walked up until their noses were an inch apart. "What did you just say?"

Jayden straightened his back, lifting his head. "No, Staff Sergeant!"

"Then don't you think that you can find something to do that might be of actual benefit to the defence of this country?"

Any leniency for the ills of those with African American heritage hadn't trickled into the army way of doing things yet, Jayden lamented.

"Yes, Staff Sergeant!"

"Well then…MOVE!"

Jayden considered saluting before scurrying off. After joining, he had found it infuriating to be belittled by a white man who by all appearances would have placed his feet on the red-neck side of the fence whenever the opportunity presented itself. But judging a book by its cover was not always an accurate endeavour. One night, on temporary leave, Jayden had got himself into a tight spot with some real red-necks in a bar just outside the base. They were well on their way to giving him a good ass kicking, when by some miracle, the Staff Sergeant walked in on the festivities. His strength was the talk of the base and Jayden soon found out why. He threw one red-neck over the bar and another through the door (which was closed at the time) before the rest of them decided that this wasn't such a great idea after all. He took Jayden back to the base and cleaned him up, hardly uttering a word the whole time. He was a hard-ass, but Jayden knew that if the shit ever hit the fan, this was the guy he wanted in his corner. Withers wasn't bluff and bravado. He was the real deal.

Jayden noticed Corporal Heche doing little around the back of the M777. He decided to both enlist his assistance and save him from a lecture.

"Come on, Heche. Give me a hand with those shells before the Staff Sergeant tears you a new one."

Jayden wasn't sure if it was respect for the rank, or just fear of the man, but when Withers was referenced, Heche jumped into action. Not that it mattered. Jayden needed help, and he just got to tell a white boy to do it. It was all good.

The monster was shallow, now a few feet under the surface. It was night, and the darkness made it feel more secure. It continued to rise until it broke the surface.

In the distance, lights of civilization twinkled. A lot of lights. Whatever this was, it seemed to be a suitable target for the acquired power and rage, which had become the monster's focus.

It was too far away to get a detailed view, but that could be remedied. The powerful tail swung up and down, moving it closer. It would observe and analyze first—destroy whatever was in its path second. The monster would be patient, waiting until it was confident that the attack would be effective before revealing itself. It sensed that this was the safest method of approach.

Once it had reached a point seven miles offshore, with the target coming into clear view, another sound caught its attention. From the north, a freighter approached, its motor chugging rhythmically. Not certain what this was, the monster did know it was a matter that had to be dealt with, and it was already experienced when it came to sinking ships.

Jayden woke fast and frightened, with no idea why. In the other cots, the rest of the section was stirring, as well. In the midst of darkness, hidden by the night, something unknown had just occurred.

He rolled out, going to the door of the tent without bothering to pull on his pants. Odds dictated that it was something banal like a distant lighting strike, shocking him from his slumber. It should be easy enough to ascertain that everything was fine so they could all get back to dreaming. He stepped onto the wet grass feeling the cool night air envelope him.

Heche stepped out taking a position standing beside him. "Hey Davis. What's going on?"

"I don't know," Jayden said. "Shut up for a minute and listen."

From their elevated vantage point, a softly glowing wall of fog was visible rolling into the Bay. It looked kind of cool, Jayden decided. Above it, stars twinkled in a clear sky. So much for the lightning theory. The city was lit up and presented well, thanks in part to the rolling topography upon which it stood. At least the scenery was nice.

"I don't hear nothing," Heche said, like a graduate student offering final defense of their thesis. At least in his mind, that was that.

"Great. Go back to bed, then."

"What're you doing?"

"If it's any of your business," Jayden snipped, "I'm going to take a quick whiz."

At that instant, a sound wave hit them. To Jayden, it sounded like someone had dropped an anvil into an empty steel drum about the size of Mount Everest. The vibration wall pushed both of them back, causing them to stumble before regaining their feet.

Heche was wild eyed with panic. "What was that?" He screamed the question in a high-pitched voice.

Jayden grabbed him by the shoulders, forcing him to stand steady. "Relax, man. Get a grip."

Heche's voice dropped off to almost nothing. "Was it an explosion?"

Staff Sergeant Withers materialized out of the gloom, fully dressed, looking like he'd been up for hours.

"Alpha Section!" His voice boomed through the air. "On your feet! Be ready to deploy in two minutes."

A chorus of grumbling and mumbled questions was audible from inside the tent.

"Davis. You and Heche might want to put on some clothes."

"Yes, Staff Sergeant." Jayden ducked back in through the doorway. At this point, sleep was pushed to the back burner. He wanted to know what was going on. In that, he was not alone.

"All right, let's go!" Withers might have cut the two minute prep time short, but nobody was going to call him on it. "Standard deployment, ladies. Let's get that Howitzer ready!"

Davis hoped this was just protocol, not an actual usage scenario for the big gun. Firing it from this proximity to a major population center was unprecedented, as far as he knew.

"Davis! Get your shit together, man! Grab those night vision goggles and get them focused on the water. Tell me what's going on out there."

"Yes, Staff Sergeant."

They were heavy and complicated, but Jayden had been well trained on using them. This was one of his specialities. He lifted them, steadied his hands, and instructed them to auto-focus. Small servos began to whine as adjustments were made, and a glowing green view of the Bay came into view. Jayden began a methodical search of the horizon.

"Anything?"

"Yeah," Jayden said, with uncertainty in his voice. He hadn't expected to see anything noteworthy.

"Well," the Sergeant replied, "what is it?"

"Something's burning."

"What do you mean *something*? Give me details, Davis."

"It's out past the Bay, on the open ocean. Range shows eight point three miles from our position. I see open flames, but not a lot. I can't make out enough details to give an accurate identification. From what I can tell, I would say it's a ship."

"A ship? Are you sure?"

"Pretty sure, Staff Sergeant. And I think she's sinking."

The Sergeant hesitated for a moment. "Take your bearings and confirm that distance. The rest of you, load that Howitzer!"

"Sir?" Jayden lowered his voice. "We can't fire on an unknown ship when it's already in distress."

"I have no intention of firing on the ship, Davis. But we might have to fire on whatever attacked it, if that's what happened. Your bearings will at least give us a starting point."

Jayden realized he was scared. "Yes sir."

Withers stalked away. "Where's that radio? I've got a call to make."

Ten minutes went by without anything happening and Davis had calmed down some. Maybe this wasn't as bad as he thought. The ship might have experienced some sort of malfunction that caused an on-board explosion.

Withers pointed. "Ten o'clock, Davis. What is that?"

Jayden focused in on the small, twinkling light in the sky. "It's an Apache, sir. It seems to be approaching the disabled ship." This was a disturbing revelation. The Apache wasn't a rescue bird. Heavily armed, it was designed for an attack role.

"Is the ship still burning? Can you see flames?"

Jayden adjusted his aim. "Yes sir. But they're fading."

If the ship was sinking, this was not a surprise. It couldn't both burn and take on water indefinitely.

"Staff Sergeant?"

"What is it, Davis?"

He lowered his voice. "What about a rescue, sir? The Apache can't pull survivors out of the water."

"No, but it can fly a lot faster than any rescue vehicle can. It's no surprise it's first on scene. Don't give up, Davis. Help will be on the way."

That made him feel better. "Yes sir."

"Keep an eye on that chopper. Yell if anything happens that I should know about."

"Yes sir." Jayden refocused both the binoculars and his attention. The helicopter was indeed moving in fast. But not for long. "Sir, the Apache appears to have reached the ship. It's hovering now."

"Okay. Keep your eyes on it."

The monster broke the surface, infuriated by the clatter of the low flying chopper. Water had already been pressurized inside its bladder, the proboscis fully extended. It fired a narrow stream of high pressure water at the hovering aircraft. It was an easy shot.

The pilot saw it coming but didn't have any time to react. It hit with tremendous force, like a gigantic fist, punching the chopper sideways, its fuselage splitting into pieces.

"Staff Sergeant!" Jayden screamed.

Withers read the emotions behind his response and didn't like them at all. "Let's have it, Davis. What do you see?"

"The Apache, sir! It took a hit. It's gone down."

The Sergeant's voice rose, but stayed steady. "Are you sure?"

"Yes, Staff Sergeant."

"You keep monitoring the area, Davis. I've got another call to make."

"I apologize for this, Mr. President." The Admiral wasn't feeling as regretful as his words may have indicated, but was following standard procedure.

The President at least had his robe tied closed. He strode along at a remarkable pace.

"Oh sure, Bill. Don't worry about it. Apparently *all* the really important and interesting things happen in the middle of the night. Who needs sleep anyway?"

I could sure use some, the Admiral thought to himself. "Exactly, sir."

"Give me the condensed version while we're walking, Bill. No point in wasting time."

"It's San Francisco, sir. We just had an Apache shot down along the coast."

"Damn! Is it that monster thing again?"

"We don't have confirmation yet. This happened just a few moments ago."

"What's your best guess, then?"

"I would say yes, it's likely the same creature."

"Son of a bitch! At least we were smart enough to move assets down the coast. Are we shooting at it?"

The Admiral frowned. "We're trying to find it. Once again, it appears to be under water."

The President stopped. He pointed a finger at the Admiral to emphasize his point. "I've had it, Bill. No more screwing around. You get assets in the air, or in the water, or on the land if that helps. You do it now. Then I want shots taken. If you even suspect that thing might be in a certain area, I want you to light it up. Let's show this son of a bitch we mean business."

"I'll authorize on site discretion, sir. All restrictions off."

"Great. Just don't shoot any of our own stuff in the process."

"Of course, Mr. President."

The Commander-in-Chief resumed walking. "Well, come on then. Let's see what the rest of those lackeys have to say."

The Admiral felt into step beside him with an effort. "Yes, Mr. President."

12

Aya managed to fall back asleep. It happened at the kitchen table, and somehow he'd been unaware of the process. He would have stumbled back to bed if he'd realized what was happening. Instead, he now sat slouched forward, his head on his forearm. He snored a little, but he was also unaware of that. Besides, he had bigger issues. He was having another dream that was transitioning into a vision.

The blackness was once again before him. He tried to move away, but to his frustration, couldn't get his legs to respond. Out of the heart of it, the monster reappeared.

It was even larger than before. The hulking abomination showed no fear. Aya was terrified that it was going to roar again, but it turned to the side, moving away. Something else had caught its attention. Aya felt tremendous relief. As the beast moved off, the ground was shaking under its weight.

Keep going, Aya thought. *Go away and never come back.*

But his relief was short lived. From the distance, where the monster was now intruding, came screams of fear, anguish and torment. Its full fury unleashed and horror fell upon the people. They were dying, Aya could sense it. Bodies were crushed, torn and rent. There was no retreat, no recourse. Death had come for them. All hope was gone. Peace was lost, only torment and affliction remained. Young, old, good, bad, all fell before the beast. Their world tumbled to the ground and was forever destroyed. The beast could not be stopped.

The chief was standing beside him. Even now, Aya was somehow aware that this was a dream, and wasn't surprised. What the chief said, however, caught him off guard.

"You can stop it."

Aya leaned back his head, laughing at the ridiculousness of the statement.

"Look."

The beast faced away from them. It seemed to be bracing for an attack. Aya looked, astonished by what he saw. "What is this?"

The chief stood stoically. "Watch."

The side of its body was armored, just as it had been in Aya's first vision, heavy and impenetrable. But then, the plates moved. Just once, and ever so slightly. They were hinged and could open. It was a confirmation of his first vision. Inside, past the armor, the darkness wasn't so deep. Perhaps vulnerability existed after all. They continued to move, opening further, preparing its terrible weapon. When the beast was ready, the attack resumed. So did the screams. But the weakness had been exposed.

Aya was horrified again. "What do I do?"

The chief looked at him with a steady gaze. "Only you know of this. You must go tell."

"Why me?"

"If not you, then who?"

Aya didn't have an answer.

"Go. Or you will forever hear their screams."

"No!"

Aya woke with a start, nearly falling off his chair. He looked around wild-eyed, realizing he was still in his apartment. All was quiet. All was well.

Or was it?

As sleep no longer held any appeal, he opted for the coffee he had earlier desired. One thing alone was certain at this moment. He would never participate in another sweat for the rest of his life.

San Francisco Bay was now alive with lights and noise. Jayden and the rest of the section watched in awe from their elevated position as the number of planes in the air continued to grow. The thundering roar of jet turbines and propellers was a constant background noise. From over the city, the first light of day appeared as a cool, blue slice glowing on the horizon.

"That's going to help." Withers stood impassively, keeping the rest of them as calm and focused as was possible under the circumstances. "At least we'll be able to see what we're shooting at."

"Or what's shooting at us," Jayden said under his breath.

They all strained to see any sign of the wreckage out over the water. So far, nothing was visible. There were no signs of whatever attacked the ship and the chopper.

"Staff Sergeant!" one of the gun crew yelled.

"What is it, Bailey?"

"Call for you, sir." The young man extended the microphone from the radio that was built into the control panel for the howitzer.

Withers strode over, taking the mic. Soon he was bent over, writing on a pad.

"All right, ladies. We're in business. Man your stations—I have firing coordinates."

Jayden was surprised, but he was here to follow orders, not question them.

"Davis, get those optics focused in. You're our eyes. If hearing protection is a concern, ladies, now is the time. Let's move!"

They were all brimming with questions that couldn't be asked, but he hoped the answers would solidify soon.

"Status?"

"Coordinates entered! Ready to fire, Staff Sergeant."

The 155mm round could hit a target over twenty miles away with great accuracy thanks to GPS coordination. But what where they shooting at?

"Shoot the damn thing," Withers hissed.

"Firing!"

Most bent over, looking away, trying to cover their ears.

The M777 put on a most impressive display. Smoke and fire belched from the barrel accompanied by a tremendous roar. The entire weapon was rocked by the recoil and the ground trembled.

Jayden focused his concentration in time to see the shell strike. A quick flash, followed by a plume of water flung skyward by the explosion was visible through the optics.

"Explosion, Staff Sergeant."

The sound of it rumbled in from the ocean.

"What else, Davis? Any sign of our target?"

Jayden had no clue what he was looking for, but the answer would have been the same regardless. "Nothing, Staff Sergeant."

"Keep looking. The rest of you, reload that weapon!"

As the rest of the section scrambled, Jayden saw something that would forever change his life. A black vision of doom arose from the water's surface. It was immense, that was clear even from a distance. It was moving inshore, the wake it was creating curling and breaking into white foam ahead of its progress. Jayden found himself incapable of responding. He had never seen anything like it, even in his worst nightmares. He had no idea what it was, but the mere sight of it filled him with enough dread to drain his strength away.

He had one thought sustain him as his coping mechanisms floundered.

His eyes had failed him.

It couldn't be real.

Withers, despite the myriad of things unfolding around him, was ever the sponge for absorbing even the most mundane details. He noticed how Davis had adopted a rigid, upright posture. Then he saw the expression on his face.

"Davis! What do you see out there?"

"I…have no idea, Staff Sergeant."

Such a useless generalization warranted a sharp response, a rebuke capable of changing a young man's attitude to be more in-line with the Army way of doing things. It was on the tip of Withers tongue when he allowed his eyes to flicker across the horizon. Even without the aid of magnification, he could see the monster approaching.

"What the hell? Davis, give me those goggles." He plucked them from limp hands, focusing on the creature. Astonished, there was no precedent or explanation for what came into his view. Whatever that was, it shouldn't be here. Withers had no idea how it had come into this world, but he had a plan for how to take it out.

"Davis! Snap out of it! Take these back and get us firing coordinates."

The task seemed to give him new life. "Yes, Staff Sergeant!"

"The rest of you! Prepare to fire."

Jayden pointed, the expression on his face reflecting horror. "Staff Sergeant! I think it just fired in our direction!"

A rippling pressure wave was flying across the ocean towards the Bay, leaving a discernable distortion on the surface of the water.

Withers knew the potential life and death value of split second decisions. He made one at that moment.

"Hit the dirt! Everybody down!" He dropped, lying flat, hoping the rest followed suit.

Jayden tried to be careful with the optics as he dropped, managing to take a good hit in his unprotected ribs as he did so. He cursed under his breath, waiting for whatever was about to happen. In a temporary, anticlimactic moment, all was quiet and peaceful. Then he heard a soft sound, like a breeze rustling through the leaves of a shade tree. It grew, however, until it was more like the moaning wind of a winter blizzard.

The wave struck. Jayden felt like someone had driven a golf cart over his back at high speed. It took his breath away. He heard various things falling over and tumbling about the site. Of course, Withers was up first after the attack.

"Alpha Section, on your feet! Is everyone all right?"

They were, but several of them had bleeding from the nose.

"Davis, update those firing coordinates! Prepare to engage." Despite minor damage around the site, the gun itself seemed unaffected by the pressure wave.

Jayden wanted to scan the city to see if there were any visible effects from the attack, but knew he had a priority job to do. In the midst of everything, he realized the sound of aircraft had gone silent. The black abomination, meanwhile, continued to move towards the Bay.

"Mark your round!" Withers cried.

"Coordinates as follows," Jayden said, followed by the necessary information.

"Target is moving inbounds," Withers yelled. "Correction of minus two degrees."

The adjustments didn't take long to enter in the digital control panel. "Ready, Staff Sergeant!"

"Fire!"

Once again, the Howitzer roared, spewing smoke and fire.

Jayden watched with anticipation, but the round hit in front of the target.

"Round was short, Staff Sergeant."

"Fire again. No adjustment. Original bearing. Target still moving inbounds."

The big gun fired again. Jayden squinted to sharpen his focus.

"Hit! Direct hit!" A visible explosion rocked the front of the monster.

"Damage report, Davis. What can you tell me?"

The ebony vision of doom was still plowing towards them, showing no signs of hesitation.

"No visible signs of damage. Target is still inbound."

Withers was stunned. "Are you sure, Davis?"

Jayden lowered the optics, spinning around to face him. "It just fired again! Incoming, Staff Sergeant!"

"On the ground, men! Get as flat as you can!"

The attack was different this time. The wave came faster, hitting harder. The monster's focus narrowed, and it fired towards the source of the artillery shell that had struck it.

When it passed over, Jayden scarcely noticed the sounds of destruction the wave was causing. He felt like a giant had stepped on his back, pressing down with all its weight. As the agony ramped up with light speed, Jayden passed out.

Aya walked into Sergeant Taft's office with purpose, but no real plan. He had heard about the attack on San Francisco while driving in, noticing a grim expression on every face he saw along the way. Details were preliminary and sketchy, but nothing coming out of the Bay area so far had been in any way encouraging.

"Good morning, Aya." Taft's voice was monotone and subdued.

"Bill, I need to talk to the Governor." There it was, laid out and clear. No time or opportunity to second guess himself and change his mind. Besides, time was of the essence.

Taft gave him a look that was sceptical at best. "I beg your pardon?"

Aya collected himself. "Bill, I know you're going to think I'm nuts—and you won't be the only one on this day. But I need to have a way to communicate to whoever is in charge of the military response to this thing, and I imagine they're in the White House or Pentagon. The Governor is the only person I can think of that might be able to open those doors."

Taft gave no response.

"I'm asking you to take a huge step of trust on this one, Bill. If you can get the ball rolling, I can take it from there. That way you have minimal exposure to what might be a terminal career move."

"I think," Taft said, "you'd better close my office door and explain yourself."

Aya closed the door, so as not to attract attention from the rest of the staff. "Bill, I know how to stop this thing."

Taft was pursing his lips as if he was sucking on a sour candy. "Well, wouldn't that be good news. But I don't see how that's possible. Just because you were in on the investigation of the attack on Malhulik, you're not an expert on this thing...whatever it is. You don't know any more about it than I do. Hell, you've never even seen the damn thing."

"But I have, Bill."

"When?" Taft spit out the question.

Now came the really big hurdle. "I've had visions."

Taft's eyebrows went up. "Visions?"

"Yes." *No hesitation, no retreat*, Aya thought. "Two of them."

Taft turned away, looking out his office window at nothing in particular. "You had visions."

"Yes. I went for a sweat, which brought them about."

"Would that be like me saying I had a dream?"

"It's more than that. I know how to stop it, Bill. This is life or death important."

Taft spun around to face him. "Aya!" He regained his composure with an effort, his voice dropping off. "You know I both like and respect you. You're a good trooper, no question about it. And I respect your heritage. Indigenous ways sometimes confuse me, but that doesn't mean they're wrong. However, if you think I'm calling the Governor to tell him that one of my troopers has had a dream about this monster, then you couldn't be more wrong."

Aya placed his hands on the desk top, leaning in closer. "They need this information to stop it, Bill. People are dying."

"Aya, I know this is upsetting. No disrespect intended, but I'm certain you're not the only person having nightmares...or dreams or visions, or...whatever you want to call them. I understand. You always have been a sensitive man, and that's a good thing." Taft sighed. "Let the military do their job. This is what they do. They're very good at it. Besides, I imagine all they have to do at the end of the day is to keep shooting bigger stuff at it until it rolls over and dies."

"In the middle of a major population center?"

Taft's tone turned defensive. "No. Of course not. Run it out of town first. Then hit it with all we've got. Nukes if it comes down to that. Even this thing couldn't survive that."

Aya pondered the implications. "Wouldn't that make us the monster?"

Taft's countenance darkened. "Look, Aya. If you can't get your shit together, then go home and work this out. I understand. We'll call it a sick day. But no more of this *call the Governor* nonsense. I have lots of work to do, and so do you."

Aya met his gaze and held it. "Final answer?" He regretted sounding like a game show host, but kept his expression impassive.

"Yes. Now go—either home or to work. But go. Any more of this talk and our relationship is going to start deteriorating."

Aya nodded, walking away. This was a disappointment, but not a surprise. Not even close to feeling like he should give up, the question was where did he go from here?

"Davis?"

The voice was both familiar and tinged with concern. Jayden opened his eyes, the final commitment to returning to consciousness.

Sergeant Withers, blood running out of his nose, looked at him with a serious expression.

"There you are. Can you get up?"

Jayden had no idea. He tried to remember what led to him being in this position in the first place. He was either numb or uninjured, because he couldn't feel any pain. He decided to give a good, military answer. "Yes, Staff Sergeant. Can you give me a hand?" Wither's arm extended, strong fingers curling around his own.

"Here we go," Withers said as he pulled.

Jayden concentrated for the initial moments of being upright on not losing his balance and falling back down again.

"You feel all right?"

Jayden nodded. "Yes sir." He started to look around. "Oh my God." The site was chaos. Even the Howitzer was on its side. Far worse, all the other men lay on the ground, unmoving. "What about the others?"

Withers frowned. "You're the only one I've been able to revive, so far."

Jayden didn't know that at least three of them didn't have a pulse. He would get that bad news soon enough. Still woozy, he found his thoughts disjointed. "What happened, sir?"

"We were attacked, remember?"

"Attacked?" His mind began to clear.

"Yeah," Withers said. He turned, looking out over the Bay. "By that."

Jayden followed his gaze. Now his memory jolted back in focus. The monster, gargantuan and black, was approaching the Golden Gate Bridge. It was both easier to see, and harder to tolerate. "God. Now I remember."

Withers put his hands on his hips, glaring.

"Staff Sergeant, where are the planes? Why aren't we fighting back?"

"That thing has an attack that seems to be as broad as the horizon. I think it knocked them all out of the air."

As if on cue, the monster stopped, firing at the bridge. The shimmering wave was visible, narrow and focused. It didn't appear to be aimed in their direction, for which Jayden was thankful. But in that moment, he felt fear and concern for the bridge and those on it.

It struck with catastrophic consequences. A cloud of metal, wire and concrete flew into the air. The wave appeared to have sliced through the structure with ease. Jayden was sure he saw at least one car tumble through the new opening, falling with great speed into the water below.

"Damn, Staff Sergeant! We've got to do something."

Withers remained impassive. "I'm sure reinforcements are on the way, Davis. But as for us, except for small arms, we've got nothing to fight back with. The big gun is trashed. I don't think a rifle is going to cut it."

"But that thing is going to destroy the bridge. There must be hundreds of people on there."

Withers figured it was more like thousands. "I know. Davis, if you've got any bright ideas, I'd love to hear them."

From their position, they could see the monster turning to line up for its next shot.

"SAM's, Staff Sergeant. There are some missiles stored under the control console."

Withers nodded. "Okay, at least you're thinking. But we already hit that thing dead on with the Howitzer. It didn't even flinch. Those missiles pack a much smaller punch than the big gun does. Besides, you'd never hit it from here. You'd be more likely to damage a sail boat or the bridge itself. I can't imagine that thing has a heat signature after splashing around in the Bay, so there'd be nothing to lock on to."

A second shimmering wave raced across the Bay. The center portion of the bridge was blown away. Moments later, large sections began to collapse and fall into the water below. It was an unprecedented disaster unfolding before their very eyes.

Jayden grimaced. "Look—based on what we're seeing, doesn't it seem likely that it's moving towards the city itself?"

Withers nodded. "That's what it did in Vancouver." He reflected on a most unpleasant thought. "I hear it eats people."

Jayden almost grabbed him, but fought off the impulse. "Then let's load up the SAM's, take the truck and head it off. Maybe we can get to the waterfront before it does."

The end result didn't seem promising, but Withers was also a man of action. Doing anything was more appealing than doing nothing. "All right. It's a start. Maybe a better idea will present itself along the way. Let's load them up and get moving."

Jayden, despite every desire to the contrary, hesitated. "What about the others?"

Withers couldn't stop himself from reacting, looking like he had been punched. "I don't know what to do with them, Davis. We can send help as soon as it's available. I imagine they'll be as safe here as anywhere."

Jayden nodded. "Okay. I mean, yes Staff Sergeant."

Withers started walking towards what was left of the Howitzer. "Come on, Davis. Let's get this shit show on the road."

13

Aya sat in his cruiser in the police parking lot, knowing it was a perilous location for making this particular call. But desperate times called for desperate measures and he didn't want to waste any time. Someone answered after one ring, catching him unprepared.

"Yes, hello. This is Corporal Aya Chee of the Alaska State Troopers calling."

The voice wanted to know how to direct his call.

"I need to speak to the Governor, please."

The female voice responded smoothly. "I'm sorry. The Governor is unavailable. Is he expecting your call?"

At least he hadn't been dismissed. Aya had already determined that despite desperate circumstances, he would not lie to get what he wanted. He would go as far as mild manipulation, but only if necessary. He chose his words carefully.

"No, he isn't. I wouldn't have called directly, but this matter is very time sensitive."

"I can create a notice and put it on his calendar. He checks that regularly. May I ask if this is a police matter?"

"This is more a matter of national security."

"Oh, I see. You said you were with the Alaska State Troopers?"

"That's correct. I'm stationed out of Anchorage." The fact that he was acting on his own didn't have to enter the conversation. If she jumped to a conclusion, that was not his fault.

"Let me take down your contact information, all right?"

"Certainly."

"Could you repeat your name and rank for me, please?"

Aya spelled it without being asked.

"All right. So what is the purpose of you call, Corporal?"

"It's…regarding the attack going on in San Francisco. I have information that could be helpful to the Defense Department."

"Really? Well, that would be good news. May I inquire as to why you are calling the Governor about this?"

"I need a contact who can pass this on to whoever can use it."

"Okay. Well, the Governor could help with that. He's in a meeting right now, but let me make this a priority. I'll pass this on as soon as possible. Will you be available at this same number?"

"Yes. This is my work cell."

"Good. Thank you for your call. I'll do the best I can with this."

"Thank you." He hung up, feeling a thread of hope. He had either taken a step closer to passing on his message, or been given a permanent dismissal by someone who was really good at it. He couldn't tell the difference. Time would reveal all.

Withers chose to drive the truck himself, racing as fast as he dared on the city's winding streets. This left Jayden free to look out over the Bay, monitoring the movement of the monster. As far as he could tell, the bridge was, for all intents and purposes, gone. Its history, practicality and recognition as a symbol of the city had all just come to an end. And that didn't take into account all the people who fell with it into the deep waters.

"How well do you know the streets, Staff Sergeant? I can track us on my phone if you want."

"Don't bother. Keep your eyes on that thing as best you can. If you can come up with a more detailed plan for stopping it, that would also be nice."

Jayden didn't have any hope for stopping it. If jets, helicopters and a direct hit in the face from their Howitzer didn't even slow it down, then nothing they had with them in the truck was going to do any better. But it would sure feel good, even as his last act if it came down to that, to blast it with a shoulder launched missile from close range. The rest of his future and all the plans that went with it had all evaporated in the face of this new reality. He acknowledged the thought, and to his surprise, he was okay with it.

"It's a good day to die, Staff Sergeant."

"You mean for us or it?" Withers had a look of surprise on his face.

"Either way. Let's get down there and make this thing eat a SAM for breakfast."

Withers spun the wheel as the truck squealed around a tight bend. "Give me a few more minutes, Davis, and I'll make your dreams come true."

Jayden had deduced that the monster was moving inland at a faster pace. They would be lucky to cut it off.

"I think it might get ashore ahead of us, Staff Sergeant."

"Then we'll chase its ugly ass through the streets until we get a clear shot."

Jayden smiled despite everything. "Very good, Staff Sergeant."

There was no longer any need to roust the President. He, as well as all other senior staff, were camped out in the Situation Room, watching in real time as the attack unfolded. Or at least they had been until the cameras were knocked out. Now there was a mad scramble to re-establish communications. The President had been unusually quiet, watching it all unfold with surprising stoicism. That couldn't last.

"Bill, come here."

The Admiral had his plate heaped with urgent tasks, but the President was the President. He pulled himself away, walking over to the Commander-in-Chief. "Yes sir?"

"Let's have a quiet, little confab just between the two of us, all right? Everybody else seems to be distracted at the moment."

"Whatever you say, Mr. President." The Admiral did a fine job of keeping his voice and face impassive despite his frustration with the interruption.

"Bill, you and I just saw the same thing, right? All our aircraft have been knocked out of the sky. We have no functional naval assets left in the immediate area. And we've lost communication with all of our land based troops. Is that a good summary?"

"Yes, Mr. President." What else was there to say?

"Take all the binders off, Bill. No restrictions—no holding back. Let me hear it straight up. What have we got left as an option to deal with this?"

The Admiral hadn't wanted it to come down to this. He knew where the President was going.

"Back up forces are moving towards the area as fast as possible."

"More of the same, huh? That's not too encouraging, Bill."

"There's also a contingent of subs moving to the area. I suspect sonar will track this thing. Torpedoes should do serious damage to it."

"Unless you hit it in the side, or if it comes ashore before they get here."

"Well, we still have all the big assets available. Two-stage bombs, MOAB's and nukes. The problem with all of those is that this battle is on our soil. The collateral damage in a population center, would be tremendous. And we all know the side effects from using a nuke."

The President pondered the implications. "None of the small stuff works and the big stuff is too dangerous. So what do we do? Wave the white flag and let it eat San Francisco?"

The Admiral hated indecision, but knew he was up to his neck in it. "I don't know, Mr. President."

"Okay. You do know that once this city is devastated, the next stop along the coast is the City of Angels. I think we need to have a contingency plan, and we need to come up with it right now."

"What did you have in mind, sir?"

The President leaned forward, closing the gap between them. "I'll tell you what I have in mind. Once the San Francisco attack is over and this thing starts to move on, we blast it with everything we've got. And I mean everything."

The Admiral didn't respond.

"Look," the President said, "planes, choppers, ships and artillery aren't working. We're up against the wall here, Bill. We can give the subs a shot assuming it goes back in the water, but based on our results so far, I'm not convinced that would resolve our problem. I'll be damned if that thing is going to reach Los Angeles."

A tall man in an elaborate military uniform strode over, emotion showing on his face. Protocol went out the window. "The Golden Gate Bridge is down. It's in the Bay."

The President's face showed anguish. "Well, here we go, Bill. Another taste of what's to come."

The Admiral nodded. "I'll put the plans in place, sir. When it moves off, we'll be ready."

"Good. Excellent. You do that. And somebody get those damn cameras working again!"

The flurry of activity ramped up another notch.

Aya's phone rang. The number came up as "private". He pulled off the road as quick as he could.

"Yes, hello?"

There was silence. Then a soft click. "Hello, is this Corporal Chee?"

Aya didn't think he recognized the voice, but knew who he was hoping for. "Yes, this is he speaking."

"This is Governor Haleigh returning your call."

Aya could have fainted. "Yes, good morning sir. Thank you."

"You have some information about the situation in California? Something you think might help?"

"Yes sir, I do."

"Well, thank God for that. But before we go anywhere with this, can you explain how you came to be in possession of this information?"

Aya took a deep but silent breath, calming himself. "Yes sir. You may or may not be aware, but I was part of the investigation into an attack on a village here in our own state."

"I recall something about that. Several small villages were damaged?"

"Yes sir. I was involved in investigating the first attack, on a place called Malhulik."

"Tell me what happened, please."

"Yes. First, a young man disappeared from the area around the lake. A short time later, a home was destroyed. The occupants disappeared. The following day the remainder of the village was attacked, the homes were all destroyed and most of the population killed. Only a small boy survived."

"My, that's terrible. Now, tell me how this relates to the current problem."

"I believe it is possible, perhaps even likely, that the same creature that attacked these villages is responsible for what's happening in California."

"Then why am I just hearing about this now?"

How to answer that, Aya wondered. "With a situation this strange, any conclusions could be viewed as controversial. There has been some disagreement about the findings, both from our office and the FBI, with whom we are cooperating, which has taken over the investigation. Also, revealing this to the public could have created unnecessary panic. Or at least that was the impression I got from the Bureau."

"I see." The tone of the Governor's voice was somewhat colder. "I'll have to have a conversation with them to find out where this matter stands. But the timely issue is—how can you help the military, and how can I help you to do just that?"

"Sir, I believe I know how to stop this thing. It may not be as invulnerable as it has so far appeared to be. I need to pass this information on to someone who can use it. But, I don't have any contact information."

"You're a Corporal, correct?"

Where is he going with this? "Yes sir."

"I'm just wondering why nobody with more jurisdictional power isn't aware of this information. You seem like a very entry level person for having something this potentially important bestowed upon you for distribution. No offense."

Now the truth, for better or worse. "My commanding officer, and the FBI agents I spoke with, probably walked away with differing opinions about this situation. I guess they have decided that further dispersal was unjustified."

"But is there a vulnerability or not? How could there be controversy about that?"

"I believe there is."

"You believe? But not your superior?"

"That is correct, Governor."

"Why?"

"Well, my information didn't come so much from our investigation, as it did from…"

"I'm sorry, I didn't catch all that. It came from where?"

Aya sighed. He felt it coming apart. "My tribal leader invited me to a steam, and I had a vision that revealed the weakness."

"A vision?" The excitement had gone out of his voice.

"Yes sir. That's why my superior didn't agree to pass this on."

"I see. Can you hold on for just a second? Something is happening."

"Certainly sir." This was bad. At least he had tried. Aya heard commotion in the background.

"My God. The Golden Gate Bridge has just collapsed. This thing is moving in to attack San Francisco."

Aya didn't have a response.

"Look, I don't know if this call is pure, undiluted hokum or not. But all things considered, I'm willing to do this. I'm going to put my Alaska State Defense Director on the phone. See if you can use him to get in touch with somebody down there. That's all I can do for you, Corporal."

"Thank you, sir. I appreciate it."

"Good luck." And with that, the line clicked again. Aya was back on hold.

Withers jammed on the brakes and the truck howled to a stop. Jayden didn't have to ask why. He could see it for himself.

"Damn. It beat us."

The monster, its bulk almost unfathomable when viewed from this close distance, had lumbered out of the water, crashing its way on shore. It was moving away from them, but it was not going to be hard to follow.

A broad path of damage was easily visible. The monster turned, disappearing from view behind tall buildings.

"Damn. We could sure use a break right about now." The Staff Sergeant jutted his jaw even further. "This thing might not be so easy to follow even with the trail it leaves. There's a lot of shit on the road."

Indeed, it was strewn with crushed vehicles, broken glass and debris from partially collapsed buildings. As Jayden tried to concentrate on formulating a plan on how to catch it, a sonic wave hit. The glass from the windows in the truck shattered, flying in all directions. It rocked as if hit by another driver, though there were none of those on this particular road. The sharp fluctuation of pressure gave him an immediate headache. But it could have been much worse, he supposed.

"Do you hear that?" Withers asked as he stuck his head out of the now nonexistent glass window.

"Sorry, Staff Sergeant, but my ears just popped. Hear what?"

It was now unmistakable. A deep, ominous rumble in the distance. The truck started shaking again. Jayden scanned direction of origin, seeing yet another horror unfolding.

"Shit! Staff Sergeant—that building is collapsing!" He pointed for emphasis.

An enormous skyscraper was tilting and dropping at the same time. It was at least several blocks away but the top was visible. Jayden was transfixed.

Withers reacted, a look of terror on his face. "Get out of the truck, Davis! Now!"

Jayden obeyed orders like a good soldier should.

Withers looked around wild eyed. "Come on! Follow me!"

Jayden joined him in a mad dash towards what looked to be a clothing store. Withers grabbed the door, pulling hard. It didn't as much as budge. The final thunderous crash of the building falling to the ground assaulted their ears. It took a while to begin fading away. But in its wake, Jayden heard another sound. Coming towards them was the reason for the Sergeant's alarm. A swirling, billowing cloud of dust (and who knew what else) was racing towards them, caused by the building collapse, swallowing everything in its path.

"Staff Sergeant!"

The glass in the door was cracked, but hadn't fallen out. Withers pulled out his sidearm, firing through it. A tinkling shower of shards fell to the ground. He kicked the remaining pieces clear with his boot.

"Come on! Get in here!" He moved through the opening, turning to allow his stocky build to fit. Jayden was right behind him.

"Don't stop. Get back away from the door."

They walked backwards down an aisle bordered by racks of shirts and pants. In a moment, the wall of dust swept past, obliterating everything in its path. Outside visibility was zero. A little swirled in through the gap where the glass was missing. The two of them could see nothing but a wall of airborne fallout from the collapse. As they watched, their breathing slowed.

"What now, Staff Sergeant?"

That was the question. The outside atmosphere was no doubt too toxic to breathe. The dust would destroy any engine they tried to start, and the monster was moving away faster than they could move on foot.

"I wish I knew, Davis. What do you think? You've had all the latest training. I know you're the smartest soldier in the section." Withers put his hands on his hips, staring. "You come up with a plan, Davis. Show me what you've got."

Jayden looked helpless and cornered. What kind of plan could be feasible in the midst of this mess? He looked around as if there might be an answer hanging on one of the racks. All he saw was the latest fashions at low, low prices.

14

The conversation with the Defense Director had gone well for one simple reason—he had not bothered to ask where the information Aya wanted to pass on had come from. The Director had assumed it was legitimate since the request to talk to the trooper had come from the Governor himself. Therefore, he had been as helpful as possible.

Now Aya sat in a variety store parking lot in his cruiser, his phone stuck to his ear, suffering through an endless number of referrals from one office to another. It was like trying to get assistance by calling a company directory. His call was important to them, but not to the extent that anybody who could help was going to bother to talk to him. Aya had no way of knowing how close he was to speaking to someone who could use this information. His phone clicked again, indicating yet another step had been taken.

"Yes?"

That was all they had to say. No introduction or formalities at all. Aya hesitated. Everyone he had spoken to so far had been polite and formal. In the background he heard multiple overlapping conversations and other sounds.

"Who is this?" the voice demanded.

"This is Corporal Aya Chee from the Alaska State Troopers. Who am I speaking to?"

His question was ignored. "How did you get on this line?"

"I was directed here by...um...the office of the assistant to the Defense and Appropriations Committee Undersecretary."

"Why?"

"I need to talk to somebody about the attack in San Francisco."

"And you're a Trooper from the State of Alaska?"

"Yes, that's right."

"Calling about the San Francisco attack?" The skepticism was obvious.

"Yes."

"Look, we're really busy right now. Maybe you should call back another time."

"The monster attacked us here first. I investigated one of those attacks."

There was a brief moment of nothing but background noise. "Okay. So what?"

"I know how to stop it."

This time the pause was longer. "Are you serious? Or is this some sort of prank?"

"I'm serious. That's why I'm calling. The Director of Defense for the State of Alaska referred me, which is how I managed to get through to you."

"Okay. How about I give you ten seconds to explain. Then, I have to go."

Aya decided to get straight to the point. "It has a weakness. And I know what it is."

"Great. You know what? If I pass this call on and you turn out to be some sort of nut job, I'm going to either get fired or at the very least, transferred to Alaska myself."

Aya struggled with his response. "I'm serious."

"And to think this isn't even close to the strangest thing I've heard today. Hold on."

The phone became muffled, sounds blurred and incomprehensible. *What just happened*, Aya wondered. Then, another voice.

"Who is this?" The voice was loud and demanding—so familiar, yet, in that moment, Aya couldn't identify it.

"My name is Aya Chee," he explained for the umpteenth time that day. "I'm an Alaska State Trooper."

"Let's just stick to the pertinent stuff. You say you know how to stop this thing?"

Aya figured out the voice. It couldn't be! "Um, yes. It has vulnerability."

"Well, for God's sake man, don't keep that kind of information to yourself. Spit it out! What are you waiting for?"

"As you wish, Mr. President." Aya never thought he'd be saying those words. "The plates on its side have a weakness."

"Are you serious or crazy? We've already hit it with everything we've got, but haven't so much as made a scratch."

"The plates themselves seem to be indestructible. But when it attacks, it has to open them up. That's when it's vulnerable."

"Are you kidding me? We've seen it attack multiple times. There was no sign of the plates opening up. Are you some kind of crank?"

"No, sir. The plates only open from behind, and not all that far. I think they're hinged, acting like a bellows to build up pressure for the attacks."

The phone was now picking up a lot more noise. Aya figured it had been put on speaker mode.

"Did you hear that, Bill? What do you think?"

Another close voice came through. "I don't know, Mr. President. We haven't taken a good look at it from behind yet. Things have been too chaotic. It could be worth investigating."

"Right. Time is of the essence, Bill. If we're going to do this, we're going to need a plan."

There was more mumbled noise.

"Listen," the President bellowed. "Thanks for the call. We'll try to use this if we can. I've got to go. Things are happening right now."

The line clicked, going dead. Aya pulled it away from his ear, marvelling at what had just happened. Realizing how uncomfortable he was from sitting so long, he stretched and squirmed in his seat. He ran a hand through his hair and let out a long sigh.

He had done it. The information was passed on.

Now he could only hope he was right.

The most frustrating thirty minutes of their lives passed. Being trapped in the store, incapable of doing anything, while the monster continued its path of destruction was terrible beyond description. The dust now seemed to be thinning out.

"Staff Sergeant? The dust is settling."

Withers squinted as he looked outside. "It is. But who knows what kind of poisons are still in the air."

"Sir, we're in a clothing store. Maybe we can find a suitable material for use for a temporary face mask."

Life crept back into Withers' eyes. "Maybe. Even if it's just good enough to get us back to the truck. There's proper breathing apparatus in the back. Goggles and headgear, too. That would get us mobile again."

"I'll go, sir."

Withers was anxious to get moving too, but didn't like the idea of sending the kid out in this alone. It didn't make sense for both of them to put themselves at risk, however; at least until they knew more about the dangers of going outside. They had reached the point where they had to do *something*.

"All right. Let's find you a temporary mask. Then you go get the breathing apparatus, goggles and headgear—nothing else. We can go out again after we're properly suited up to grab the missiles and a radio."

"You don't think the truck is drivable, Staff Sergeant?"

He sighed. "I doubt it, Davis. It has a good filter system, though. I suppose it might be worth a try. Maybe I need to look at the big picture. If we wreck it, so what? That's just one more small thing to add to a large list."

Yes, Sergeant."

They found a shelf full of scarves. Jayden selected one, (more for appearance than for any practical reason), tying it around his nose and mouth.

"I think this will work, Staff Sergeant." His voice was muffled.

Withers knew that different particulate matter needed specific types of material to filter it out. This approach would stop the largest dust particles, but not the smaller, more dangerous ones. But, today was a day for risks.

"All right. Make it quick. If you have any trouble breathing, or see any other signs of danger, get back here fast."

"Yes, sir."

Jayden hesitated in the doorway for an instant. In truth, he could already sense that he was breathing in some of the dust. He concentrated on not coughing in response. If he did, Withers might call him back in. He walked off with steady strides towards the truck, amazed at how this little part of the world had changed so much in such a short period of time. Everything was coated with a thick layer of dust, even the ground he walked on. An eerie silence hung in the air; he heard no sounds whatsoever. Even his own footsteps were muffled to a whisper. Jayden narrowed his eyes to slits in the hope of reducing the amount of junk that was getting into them. He reached the truck without incident, opening up the back tailgate. At least the inside was clean. He jumped up to take advantage of the shelter, climbing in.

Withers must have been concerned about the welfare of his trooper. He assumed a look of great relief when Jayden walked back into the store.

"Got'em, Staff Sergeant," he exclaimed, whipping off the scarf.

"We're in business. Good work, Davis." Withers started to put on the protective gear.

"What now, Staff Sergeant?"

That issue Withers was still struggling to resolve. "We'll clean off the outside of the air intake for the engine, then start the truck to see if it'll run. Assuming it does, we chase after this thing."

Jayden nodded, but tried to envision how that was going to be possible. The amount of carnage generated by the monster made approaching it dangerous at best, impossible at worst. That was assuming it didn't attack them directly. "Sounds good, Staff Sergeant."

By the time they exited the store, the gear they were wearing made them look like characters in a sci-fi movie.

"Wipe off that air breather, Davis." Withers hopped into the truck.

Jayden did as instructed and was rewarded with the sound of the big engine roaring to life. He wasted no time joining Withers in the cab.

"Sounds good, Staff Sergeant!"

Withers put the truck in gear. "We'll see."

He backed up, spinning the front end around. "The streets are going to be impassable in that direction. We'll go a few blocks to the east, then try to pick up its trail again. I want to get away from this fallout anyway."

"Roger that."

The truck moved forward, kicking up dust as its speed increased. "Davis, it that radio on? Check it."

Jayden picked up the multichannel radio from the seat, concerned with the coating of dust it had on it. He brushed it off with his hand. "This radio is off, Staff Sergeant."

"Turn it on. See if you've got battery strength."

The switch clicked and the display lit up. "Radio is on, Staff Sergeant."

Chatter blared, at first indistinguishable.

"Davis! What are they saying?"

"Stand by, Staff Sergeant." With no glass in the windows, the cab was a noisy environment.

"Put out a call, Davis. Let them know we're here."

"Yes sir." He keyed the radio's transmit button. "This is PFC Davis, 49th Field Artillery Regiment, EF Company. Can anybody read me, over?"

The radio was silent. Then, a scratchy voice.

"This is Lieutenant Major Reynolds. Say again, I repeat, say again."

Davis recited his identity.

"Davis, are you part of that artillery section on Mount Hidalgo?"

"Yes sir, that's affirmative."

"What's your situation there? Are you still functional?"

"Negative. I repeat, negative. We took a direct hit. The howitzer is unusable. We have multiple men down."

"Okay, roger that. We're stretched a little tight right now, but we'll get help there as soon as possible. Tell me this—do you have eyes on the target, over?"

"Negative. My CO and I have left the site. We are on the ground in pursuit of the target, over."

"In pursuit? How can you be in pursuit?"

"We're in the section truck, sir. We are northbound approximately eight blocks from the harbor front."

"There's a lot of damage there, son. How are you able to drive?"

"We're detouring around the worst of it, sir."

"How many of you are there in total?"

"Just us two, sir."

"I see. Am I to assume that this is a recognisance mission?"

"Negative, sir. Search and destroy. We have SAM's with us in the truck."

"Son, can your CO hear me right now?"

"Yes sir. He's right beside me."

"Good. Listen up, both of you. We've taken a lot of hits from this thing. Our resources right now are very limited. It is my firm belief that you cannot take out this target with a SAM. Therefore, I am ordering you not, I repeat not, to engage the target. Do you understand?"

Jayden looked at Withers who shrugged. Orders were orders.

"Yes, sir."

"Listen to me. If you can track this thing, then do it! We can use you for updates. The information would be quite valuable to us. Do you understand?"

"Yes, sir."

"Keep this radio on. If your battery situation is bad, then turn it on every ten minutes and listen for messages. Do you have any idea how far you are from it right now?"

"No, sir. We had to take shelter when a building collapsed. We lost a lot of time."

"There's nothing else you could have done. Keep tracking it. And stay in touch."

"Roger that. Over and out."

Withers kept his eyes on the dusty road. "Turn that thing off for now, Davis. I don't think we're going to resume contact with the monster any time soon. Might as well save the battery."

"Roger that, Staff Sergeant."

The streets were abandoned. As a result, Withers kept his foot pressed hard on the gas. With no traffic to encumber their progress, the heavy military truck roared along. As the blocks flew past, the city transformed from one district to the next. It was enough to give one an appreciation for the architecture and overall scenic appeal, except for the circumstances.

The roads were seldom level or straight, and at this speed Withers was concerned about running down some distracted pedestrian (should one actually appear). He glanced over to confirm that Davis had his eyes scanning for anything noteworthy in their path. People, vehicles, debris...

Or monsters.

A lot of conversation about the plating on the monster had taken place. A plan was yet to be finalized, however. There were logistical issues.

"With all due respect, Mr. President," the Admiral said, "I don't see how we can get in a position where we can fire at this thing from behind it at the exact moment it decides to open up these plates."

"Oh come on. You're telling me that in all the recorded history of the military, there has never been a simultaneous front and back attack formation before?"

The Admiral held up his hands as if to slow things down. "Of course, flanking is a common maneuver under the right circumstances. But this thing destroys whatever is in front of it so effectively and quickly, I don't think we'd have time to move a unit into position behind it even if we did succeed in establishing a frontal attack."

The President was about to respond when CIA Director Collier walked into the room. The Commander-in-Chief's countenance darkened. "Just a minute. Collier, get over here!"

He approached, sporting just the right blend of concern and professionalism. "Good morning, gentlemen. Mr. President."

"Cut the horse shit, Collier. I've got a question for you."

"How can I help?" He assumed an expression of eager cooperation.

"What do you know about the plates on this thing?"

He blinked. "Plates?"

The President's face grew darker red. "Yeah, plates. Those things along the side of it that we can't shoot through. Do you know anything about them?"

"No. Not really."

"Is that so?"

"We've never had an opportunity to study them. A sample would be great, be we haven't had that available to us so far."

The President grew artificially calm and quiet. "They're hinged, you know." Collier blinked again. The President read his response and knew what it meant.

"Hinged?"

The President nodded, his voice still subdued. "That's right. We just found out."

"I see."

"It's a potential weakness, we think."

Collier seemed to be musing that one over. "That's hard to say."

The President shook his head. "No it's not. I just said it. Easy as pie. And by the way, Collier…while you're standing here in front of all these witnesses, is this the first time you've heard about this plates being hinged?"

He froze. It was as if he had been turned to stone.

"Go ahead, Collier," the President encouraged. "Spill it."

"One of the survivors from the Toklat crew reported seeing a phenomenon like what you're describing. We thought it might have been a mistake on their part due to the stress of the situation."

The President's face went from red to purple. "I see." For a moment, the room was quiet and nobody moved. That was when the unexpected happened. The Command-in-Chief punched Collier in the face, dropping him to the floor.

There was a collective gasp as all eyes focused on the incident. The President held up a warning finger, waving it for emphasis.

"That didn't happen!"

Everyone found something else that needed their attention. The President knelt beside the stunned man.

"You listen to me, Collier. First of all, you're fired. Take your arrogance with you and get out. I'd better never see your pathetic face again. Understand?

"Second, I want ever shred of information about this thing delivered to this room within the hour. Is that clear? Every shred. If you omit so much as one tiny detail, you're going to get invited back to a secluded place, in a quiet room, where you will get questioned about it the old fashioned way. Do you understand me?"

Collier looked for all the world like he was about to cry. "Why?"

"Why?" The President glowered. "I'll tell you why, you pathetic jerk. We had to find out about this potential weakness from an Alaska

State Trooper who somehow navigated the bureaucratic maze of our phone system to reach us. If he hadn't done that, guess what! We still wouldn't know. While citizens are dying, cities are being destroyed, and our military is being decimated, you were nestled in your office, probably looking at yourself in a mirror and thinking about how smart and wonderful you are. Who knows what other information you're holding back, even now? Frankly, you and your kind make me sick. Now get out!"

Collier stumbled to his feet, making his way towards the door. The President stared after him. "Make sure he gets escorted to his office, then to the exit. Somebody stay with him. Keep his hands off any computers. If you want to give him a kick to send him on his way, that's fine with me too."

The Admiral gestured to a lower ranking military official. "Send a couple of Marines with him."

The President stared at the Admiral. "Wait a minute. I just had an idea."

"Sir?"

"Marines. That's the ticket."

"I don't understand, Mr. President."

"You don't have to. Grab me six Marines."

The Admiral hesitated. "Which…"

"The six closest Marines. It doesn't matter which ones. I don't care about rank or service experience or any of that junk. Don't plan this or put any thought into it whatsoever. Just grab the six closest Marines and get them in here."

The Admiral stood with his mouth agape.

"Now, Bill!"

"Yes, sir."

It didn't take long to put six confused, somewhat concerned Marines before the President.

"Good. You're a fine looking group. Now, let's see…" The Commander-in-Chief looked for a clear spot at the long table before them. "Oh, the hell with it." He put his arm flat on the polished wooden surface, sliding it along, unceremoniously dumping everything onto the floor. Now the Marines looked even more concerned, and they weren't the only ones.

"Forget about that stuff," the President ordered. "Now we have some space. All of you, take a seat."

They hesitated.

"Go on. Three on this side, three on the other. I'll stand at the end so we can all hear each other."

They followed his orders, sitting.

"Perfect. Give me your last names."

There was yet another awkward pause before one of them took the initiative, starting the process.

"Johnson."

"Garcia."

"Walker."

"Morris."

"Sanchez."

"Henderson."

The President nodded. "Good." He addressed the only woman among the group. "Sanchez?"

"Yes, sir?"

He looked the group over. "You see Walker sitting there? If you were back in basic training, could you kick his ass?"

Sanchez looked terrified to answer.

"It's okay. I'm asking. Just tell me the truth."

She straightened before replying. "Yes sir!"

The President smiled. "That's better. I knew it, by the way. You have that look about you."

Sanchez fought off the urge to smile.

"Look around the room," the President said, addressing the group. "This is America's best and brightest in the field of military defense. We've gathered here to deal with this attack going on in San Francisco. We've been at it for hours. You know what we've come up with so far?"

No one answered.

"Jack shit, that's what. We're getting our asses kicked. With all our technology and cutting edge equipment—with the finest and best trained fighting men and women in the world, we haven't been able to do anything demonstrably helpful. Hell, I don't think we've even slowed it down."

The Marines were silent.

The President put his hands on the table, leaning forward. "Let me tell you why you're here. I want you six to come up with a plan for dealing with this."

A look of abject terror washed across their stoic faces.

"Relax. I know this is out of your comfort zone. Humor me, all right? I would like to know what you would do if you were put in charge of this situation."

They still looked terrified.

"Don't worry. If you suggest something impractical or stupid—we just won't do it. We're at a point where we've got nothing to lose. What better time or circumstance to call in the Marines?"

There was no response. "You can't do any worse than we already have. I don't care if you tell me to leave a warehouse full of cigarettes in front of it so that it'll take up smoking, or drop a sumo wrestler on it from Airforce One.

"I'm giving you ten minutes. Ignore everybody and everything around you. Brainstorm. Work it through. You're Marines. I know you're up to this challenge. Then we'll talk. You can fill me in on your ideas."

The President looked around the room. "If anybody interferes with this in any way, there'll be hell to pay."

There wasn't much chance of that. At this point, everybody knew the President wasn't joking.

"Oh, and one more thing. It's possible that there could be a weakness. The plating on the side of this thing opens before it attacks. It could be vulnerable from behind when that happens. I'm not sure how much value that information will be, but take it into account."

He turned, stalking off, leaving the six Marines staring at each other.

15

Withers first slowed the truck, then stopped.

"What is it, Staff Sergeant?" Jayden asked.

He shook his head. "We're getting nowhere. Hell, we don't even know where this thing is right now. We might be going in the wrong direction."

Jayden thought it through. "We're following the destruction, Staff Sergeant. We must be going the right way."

Withers grimaced. "Not if it's ten clicks from here going on a diagonal path. By the time we figure it out, it will be even further away. Or for that matter, it might be looping back towards us by now."

Jayden looked at the skyscraper beside them, an office building which appeared to be at least twenty stories tall. "Staff Sergeant?"

"What is it, Davis?"

"I bet we could see it from up there." He pointed at the building.

Withers cogitated. "I doubt there's any power for the elevator. That means using the stairs."

Jayden smiled. "I'm part of the best trained military force on the planet. It's not a problem, Staff Sergeant."

"In that case," he said, "you'd better get a move on. We can't sit here for long."

"On it, sir." Jayden jumped out, jogging towards the door, hoping it would be open.

Withers watched him enter, lamenting that he was at an age where twenty flights of stairs didn't seem very appealing. He was also aware that this would be a very bad time for the monster to return.

"Hurry up, Davis. I'm not much good at being inactive."

Jayden got on the roof, careful to prop the access door open. It would lock behind him if he didn't. That was a scenario he could live without.

He walked to the edge, letting his breathing and heart rate slow down after the long climb. To the west he saw a large plume of either smoke or dust rising into the air. He studied the view in that direction, seeing the back of the monster visible above some smaller buildings. He took a moment to estimate distance and bearing, then ran back towards the stairs.

One other thing the carnage visible from the roof confirmed—if somebody didn't stop this thing soon, there wouldn't be any city left to save.

Withers was impressed with the speed with which Davis completed his task, although he had no plans to say anything in that regard. "What did you see, Private?"

Jayden tried to control his breathing so that he wouldn't seem winded. "Found it, sir. Approximately seven clicks to the north west."

"Good job," Withers said. "That's our direction, then." He put the truck in gear, but then hesitated. "Turn that radio back on, Davis. Let's get an update."

Jayden turned it on to soft static and nothing else.

"Ring their bell, Davis."

"Yes sir." He keyed the mike. "PFC Davis here. Can you read me, Lieutenant Major?"

There was no response.

"Battery still good?" Withers asked.

"Yes sir."

"Maybe we're in a low spot."

The radio crackled to life. "Davis, this is Lieutenant Major Reynolds. I read you. What is your situation, over?"

"We just stopped to get an elevated view from a tall building. We spotted the creature seven clicks to the north west from our location."

"Good work, you two. Keep tracking it. Any other updates on the situation from your end?"

"There's a lot of damage, sir. We need to stop this thing fast or San Francisco is going to be nothing more than a memory."

"Listen up. I'm going to share some information that just came in. We're not ready to act on it yet, but it's a great reason to keep real time info on the attack. I have it from the highest sources that there may be a weakness to this thing. We haven't figured out how to exploit it, but we're working on that right now. Keep it in sight if possible. We may be able to do something about this before long. You can help us pull the trigger when the plan comes together."

"Yes, sir. Sounds good, sir."

"Save your battery. Keep checking in. Reynolds out."

Jayden shut off the radio, looking at his superior. "What do you think, Staff Sergeant?"

Withers started the truck rolling. "I hope he meant that. I've been around long enough to know that Military Intelligence can be an oxymoron. And worse, propaganda can go hand in hand with a military plan."

"If it smells like bullshit…"

Withers nodded. "Yup. It just might be. But we've still got a job to do, regardless. Keep your eyes open for anything I should be aware of. Let's go."

"Should we have a SAM up here with us, available if, you know, we can get close?"

Withers shrugged. He readjusted his death grip on the steering wheel, a look of grim determination on his face. "Naw. I've got my .45. It's probably about as useful."

Jayden found little humor in his assessment.

The President returned to the table. The six Marines stiffened their posture. They all leapt to their feet, saluting.

"Thank you. Please, take your seats."

They did, while the Commander-in-Chief analyzed their body language. He wasn't encouraged by what he saw.

"Do you all want to talk or has someone been appointed as spokesman?"

Neither option seemed to appeal to them—they all sat unmoving, even their eyes locked in looking straight ahead at nothing in particular.

"That's fine. We'll do this on a more informal basis, then. So, tell me what you've got."

No one spoke; no one moved.

"Keep in mind I invited you in. Also, I haven't forgotten what a difficult position I created for you when I did so. Let's say I'm not expecting you to present some sort of miracle right now…I'm just curious. Therefore, since there seems to be a general reluctance to talk, and since we've already spoken briefly, what do you have to say, Sanchez?"

Her expression suggested that someone had just pulled a gun on her.

"Go ahead, spill it. Contrary to what the media might suggest, I don't bite. Don't make me order you."

She was defensive and apologetic from the onset. "Mr. President, we feel like we don't have enough information to come up with a plan. Intel is essential. We have only a basic, hazy notion of what's happening on the ground. Real time info and a specific, detailed description of the enemy and its capabilities are required in order to construct a feasible strategy."

The President nodded. "Well said, Sanchez. Lacking in value, but well said. Are the rest of you in agreement that this is an accurate assessment of your conclusions?"

No one spoke, but there was nodding around the table.

"There's a reason I didn't supply you with precise Intel. We don't have it ourselves. This thing knocked out our resources so quick, there was no time to gather data. We know it's big, and getting bigger. We know it is invulnerable so far to any weapons we've used against it. And we know it seems to have an agenda based on mayhem and destruction. But that's it.

"We don't know what it is, we don't know where it came from, and we don't know how to stop it. We're fighting it blind. None of its physical characteristics are available to use against it. How does it breathe? How can it grow so fast? How much does it need to eat? Hell, we don't know how this thing takes a shit. It could expel some kind of toxic diarrhea that melts through metal as far as we know.

"It is not unique for a Marine to find themself in a chaotic, stressful situation. Think it through. Keep the possibility of vulnerability from a rear attack in mind."

This little corner of the room remained silent.

"Let's imagine this," the President said. "You just landed on a beach. The rest of your unit has been destroyed. The monster just ambled off towards your home town with a hungry look on its face. You only have the information that I just shared with you. What are you going to do? There's no time to form a committee to study this thing. You need action and you need it now. What are you going to do?"

They exchanged glances.

"Go after it?" the one named Morris said.

"Are you asking me or telling me?" the President responded.

"Telling you, sir."

"Fine. Then what?"

"Hit it with everything we've got."

"That's a perfectly acceptable plan for a Marine. I can tell you, however, that no weapon you'd be carrying would be in any way effective against it. It also seems capable of moving faster than a man can walk. Anyone else?"

The one named Walker seemed deep in thought.

"What about you, Walker?" the President said. "Got anything useful to add?"

He looked up, meeting the President's gaze. "You said the only vulnerability was from behind, and only when it was preparing to attack?"

"I more or less said that, yes. Why do you ask?"

"Okay, we got nothing else, so…split us into two groups of three. One group has to approach from behind, preparing to take advantage of the weakness. The other group has to get in front of it and somehow entice it to attack."

"Good. At least you're starting to think now. That plan occurred to us when we heard about the weakness. However, a myriad of operational shortfalls stand in the way of implementation. They include, but are not limited to, the following.

"We have minimal resources in the area right now. More are on the way, you'd better believe that—but the destruction continues moment by moment. We're losing the city while we wait. How do we get in front of it and behind it at the same time? Who can we use to do that? How do they communicate to coordinate with that sort of precision? What weapon system can we use that would be effective and still light enough to move with speed? What becomes of the team in front if the attack from the rear fails?

"That's just scratching the surface of the issues that are part and parcel with this plan. But I tell you what…how about you six assume this plan is how we have to move forward. Now start working out ways to overcome the problems standing in our way. Johnson, what's your problem? You look like you just ate something coated in crap."

"What about our posts, Mr. President?"

"Don't worry about that. Whoever you are accountable to is accountable to me. Concentrate on this project. Don't worry about anything else. Clear?"

They all nodded.

"Great. Impress me with your operational skills."

The truck stopped.

"What is it, Staff Sergeant?"

Withers looked pissed. "We're overheating." He turned off the engine. It knocked roughly before stopping. Steam emitted from under the hood and hissing was audible.

Jayden wondered what else could go wrong. "What now, sir? Wait for it to cool off? Or should I find some bottled water somewhere?"

"Naw, it's pooched. Too much dust clogging up the cooling system I guess."

They had been driving through an affluent neighborhood that had no visible signs of damage from the monster. Up until this moment, they had been making good time.

"Do we go forward on foot?"

Withers shook his head. "Not carrying those SAM's. We need another vehicle. Come on, follow me."

They trudged up a flawless concrete driveway towards a gorgeous home which Jayden figured was worth more money than he would make in his entire lifetime. Palm trees were scattered around the sprawling Spanish style mansion with a lawn manicured to perfection. Creamy stucco walls were covered by a red roof with sculpted shingles. Withers walked up as if he owned the place, Jayden following with a significant degree of reluctance. They marched up to the front door. Withers rang the bell. Beautiful chimes sounded inside the home.

The door swung open on silent hinges to reveal a woman peering at them with curiosity. She was dressed as if going to some formal event despite the early hour. Jayden pegged her age at approaching sixty, but she seemed intent on presenting herself as if much younger. It was working. He figured she could be the centerfold if Playboy had a geriatric version, but kept those thoughts to himself. He also figured she had the look of someone who was brimming with entitlement, who would likely not be open to entertaining their request.

"Can I help you?" she said, carefully annunciating her words.

"Apologies for bothering you, ma'am," Withers responded. "I'm Staff Sergeant Withers, and this is PFC Davis. We're with the 49th Field Artillery Regiment. We're part of the deployment assigned with protecting the city."

She raised one eyebrow, then lowered it again. "I'm not sure I would be bringing that to people's attention based on the news reports I've been watching."

There was no point in misrepresenting their position. "Yes ma'am. We've taken heavy loses. Our remaining resources are thin at best. That's why it is critical that Davis and I continue tracking this creature."

"I believe you. I'm not certain why you would feel compelled to check in with me about this matter, but carry on. Don't let me stand in your way."

"It's not that simple. Our truck just broke down."

"Would you like me to call the Automobile Club for you?"

"No ma'am. I would like you to lend us a vehicle."

Now both eyebrows rose, staying in that position. "You would? Tell me, Sergeant, why did you decide to knock on my particular door with this request?"

Withers gestured towards the street. "This is where we broke down."

She took a step forward, looking past them towards their truck. "I see. Do you suppose this kind of request would be covered under my insurance policy in your opinion?"

Withers cleared his throat. "I doubt it."

She smiled. "Very good. At least we have established that you are endeavoring to be honest. That is an important point."

"Ma'am?"

"What do you intend to do with the car, if I "lend" it to you?"

How to answer that? "We will continue to track, and hopefully engage this monster."

"Do you suppose my sedan will acquire a scratch or two during this process?"

Withers nodded. "It's possible."

"I see." She turned to look at Davis, whose eyes were wandering where they shouldn't have been, motivated by his appreciation of her well-kept figure accented by the revealing gown she was wearing.

"Losing our focus, PFC Davis?" she asked.

His head snapped up, embarrassment washing over him. "No ma'am!"

She seemed to be enjoying his discomfort. "That's all right, Private. If you saw what was under here, it might change your entire world view."

Withers had no idea where this was going, but knew they didn't have any time for it. "Ma'am, what about your car?"

"It's my husband's car, and therefore I shall be happy to serve my country with this small gesture. He can afford another one, and besides—I think he gives it more attention than he does me. I will open the garage door for you, Sergeant. If Private Davis would be so good as to follow me, I will get him the keys."

"Thank you, ma'am. This helps us a lot."

"And don't worry about any "scratches" you may accumulate along the way, Sergeant. Come along, Private."

They strode through an expansive room with cathedral ceilings, under an enormous chandelier, into a long, gleaming kitchen.

"I don't do much cooking, in case you're wondering. Otherwise I'd offer you a snack. Wait there." She went behind the counter, pulling a set of keys off a hook on the wall. She walked back to him, but didn't offer the keys.

"Do you have a phone, Private?"

The question threw him off. "I beg your pardon, ma'am?"

"Really, Private; I have no idea how to pose the question in a simpler manner."

"Um, yes. I have a phone."

"Are you carrying it with you?"

Why would she need a phone? She could afford one or dozens, for that matter. "Yes ma'am. I have it with me."

"May I see it?"

More confusion ensued.

"Private, this is not meant to be complicated and you are on a tight schedule, I presume. May I see your phone…please?"

"Yes ma'am." He dug through his pockets, surrendering it to her waiting hand.

"There, you see? It wasn't all that difficult, was it? Now, is this password protected?"

"Yes ma'am."

"Would you be so kind as to unlock it for me?"

Jayden had given up on figuring out what her motivation was. "Yes ma'am.

She handed it back and he entered the code.

"Very good. Hand it back to me."

Jayden complied, thinking the Sergeant was going to start yelling for him any second now.

"Where is your camera app? Oh, I see it. Now, let's just open that up." Her fingers worked the screen. "There, perfect."

She hooked one finger on the neckline of her gown, pulling it open so the front gaped. With her free hand, she shoved the phone down the opening, snapping a picture. Jayden was stunned.

"There you go, Private. And here are the keys. I suspect you'll be needing them as well."

He took both and just stood there, confused.

She responded with an alluring smile. "Don't knock it if you haven't tried it, PFC Davis. It's just something to remember me by. Now, shouldn't you be going?"

"Oh! Yes, ma'am. Thank you ma'am. For the car, I mean."

"You're welcome. For the car, I mean. And for the gratuitous photo of my breasts. That kind of work needs to be seen and admired more often than it has been. Now, run off."

The garage door was open when he went around the front of the house. Withers stood there looking impatient. He extended his hands to receive the keys. Jayden almost handed him his phone by mistake, but retracted it in a slight panic.

"Took you long enough. What were you doing in there?"

"Nothing sir!"

Inside the garage sat a huge BMW sedan, gleaming even in the shadows.

Jayden's jaw dropped. "Wow."

"Come on, Davis," Withers chided. "Let's go before she changes her mind."

This was an order that was easy to follow. "Yes, Staff Sergeant."

The monster stopped as it crested a hill during a brief respite in its quest for destruction. It had been eating less, focusing more on destroying everything in its path. The city was too large to succumb to the attack as it had unfolded thus far. It would take days to complete the carnage, but that left time for a counter-attack. A new approach came to its thoughts as it looked out over what remained of San Francisco.

It was now large enough to unleash a very broad sound wave over a large area. This elevated position was the perfect spot from which to do it. Due to its size and weight, it hesitated for a moment to ensure it had secure footing. Confident that it could absorb the recoil from a massive blast, it began to unhinge the plates along its side, pumping air, building pressure. Once the maximum was reached, the proboscis extended, fine-tuned itself, and released a tremendous blast.

The wave washed across the horizon like a tsunami, covering a 180° swath from where it was fired. At this width, it didn't have quite enough strength to knock over large structures, but damaged everything in its path to some degree. The monster sensed the success rate of the attack, determining to use it again. It scanned the horizon for another suitable position from which to fire off another round.

The Beemer was a delight to ride in, Jayden discovered. It was luxurious and the ride was so smooth, it was as if bumps and potholes didn't even exist. He tinkered with the air conditioner while Withers concentrated on driving, fine tuning it to perfection. He was also toying with the possibility of asking his superior if he could turn on the sound system.

Some movement caught his attention. He looked left towards the strip mall that they were passing. A gigantic, shimmering sound wave washed over it, peeling sections of the roof off as it went.

"Sergeant!"

The warning, coming only a split second before it hit, was of little value. The car lifted on the impact side, then crashed back down on the asphalt. The engine stalled, the glass in the windows shattering into a complex web of cracks. From all directions around them came the sounds of buildings and vehicles being damaged.

Withers, in a rare deviation, looked both shocked and afraid. "Shit! Where did that come from? Can you see the monster, Davis?"

Jayden shook his head. "No, Staff Sergeant. But the wave came from that direction."

They both looked but saw no signs of the monster.

"Do you think that was meant for us?" Jayden said.

Withers continued to look for any signs of their quarry. "I sure hope not. If that thing snuck right up on us like that, we'd be finished." He turned the key, starting the car started up again.

"There's German engineering for you, Sergeant."

Withers frowned. "The good news is it's running. The bad news is I can't see out of this shattered windshield. Give me a hand, Davis. We've got to get this out before I can drive anywhere."

They both climbed out, leaving the questionable security of the car.

16

The President strode over, no doubt expecting a report. Six Marine's looked unhappy about it.

"Okay, what have you got?"

Speculating that he would ask her first, Sanchez cleared her throat. "Mr. President, this is a very unusual situation. Also, it seems that circumstances are very fluid. The situation on the ground is unclear. Therefore we are assuming that it is changing by the moment. There is so much we don't know, so…we can only plan with the little information we have. Sir, are you able to communicate with anyone at all that is in proximity to the monster?"

The President frowned. "We have very few functioning assets at this moment. There is a small contingent from the 49th Artillery Regiment, or at least what's left of it, trying to track this thing. They have a radio and we have been able to contact them. I think to some extent the info my military people are feeding me about this is exaggerated in order to make me feel better and make them look less ineffective. So take it with a grain of salt."

She pondered. "How many troops are there in this group?"

The President looked away. "Reynolds! Get over here and I mean now!"

A tall man with a myriad of service medals on his uniform strode over. "What is it, Mr. President?"

"I need clarification regarding the troops from the 49th that are tracking the monster."

The Lieutenant Major wasn't thrilled but had no choice but to answer. "Yes, sir."

"How many men are there?"

"There are two, sir."

"Two? Why wasn't that explained? I got the impression there were more than that."

"The rest of the section was rendered inactive after an attack."

The President turned his attention back to the Marines. "Okay, so there are just two. Can you do anything with that?"

Before Sanchez could answer, Reynolds chimed in.

"Mr. President, I have been in radio contact with these men. They are following my orders to track this thing. We are working on a contingency plan. There's no need to pull these people from their post. We have things well in hand."

The President narrowed his eyes as he gave the Lieutenant Major his full attention. "Well in hand, you say? Is that how you would refer to this fiasco, Reynolds?"

"Well sir, I..."

"Shut up, you pompous nimrod! I expect you to talk when I ask you a direct question—not when you feel the urge to pontificate some drivel about how great you think you are. Your comments are bull shit! This is a cluster fuck of unprecedented magnitude. So far, the sum total of all your efforts is zilch! Don't come over here and disrespect these Marines right in front of me and not expect to get your ass kicked. Now take a hike. We can manage without you and your delusions."

He blinked in surprise. "Yes, sir."

The President turned back to the small group at the table. "You see what I have to put up with? When you folks get promoted, don't let it go to your heads. Now, give me an honest answer, Sanchez. Two troops aren't going to be able to get the job done, are they?"

She swallowed before answering. "I don't believe they are, Mr. President."

"So somehow, we have to coordinate an effort to rendezvous more troops with these two. How hard could that be under the circumstances? And that's just the beginning." He looked up, seeming to lose his focus. Then, his eyes brightened as he looked back around.

"Reynolds! Set me up with a radio. I want to talk to those two from the 49th."

Anything other than fast obedience would lead to more castigation. "Yes, Mr. President. Right away, sir."

The President looked back towards the Marines, lowering his voice. "That guy's a moron."

They struggled not to smile.

The shattered windshield now lay on the shoulder just off the sidewalk, and visibility was re-established.

"We're good to go. This might be the perfect time to tell you to stop messing with the car, Davis. We don't need air conditioning now anyway, correct?"

Jayden nodded. "Correct, Staff Sergeant."

"Turn on the radio for a minute, since we're stopped. It's been awhile since we were in contact with anybody. Maybe somebody has some news."

"Yes, sir." The switch clicked, a short burst of static following. Then nothing.

"How's the battery holding up?"

"It's good, sir," Jayden said. "Still over ninety percent."

Withers put the car in gear. "Why don't you leave it on for five minutes? After that, shut it off."

"Yes, sir." Jayden, seeing no reason not too, set the radio down in the console between the seats.

Withers seemed about to admonish him with a lecture about how important the radio was when a voice boomed out of it.

"49th Artillery Division, are you there?"

The voice was different from that of the Lieutenant Major they had talked to earlier. Jayden scrambled to pick it up.

"This is the President. Can you hear me?"

Jayden, who was about to key the mike, froze in place at this pronouncement.

"Answer it," Withers said.

Jayden looked at the radio like he was seeing it for the first time and had no idea how to use it.

"I say again, can you hear me? This is the President."

Duty called and Jayden answered. "This is PFC Davis from the 49th. I read you loud and clear."

"Thank God. I was beginning to get worried about you, son. What is your situation?"

"Our truck broke down, sir. We borrowed a civilian vehicle and are continuing to track the monster. We're in some subdivision in the northeast part of the city. The monster attacked again several minutes ago, but we're fine. We just resumed tracking. Over."

"Outstanding work. It's just the two of you?"

"That's correct, Mr. President."

"Who's your commanding officer?"

"Staff Sergeant Withers, Mr. President."

"Good. That's the perfect rank for this kind of assignment. He's not too pompous and delusional, is he?"

Jayden almost smiled as Withers gave him a quick glance. "No, sir."

"Just what I wanted to hear. Can you see the monster, son? Do you have eyes on it right now?"

"No, Mr. President. But, based on the last attack, we have a good idea what direction it is from our current location."

"Well, that's something. What is your CO doing right now?"

"Driving, sir."

"Can he hear me?"

"Yes, sir. He's sitting beside me."

"Then listen up," the President said. "There's plenty of bad news, but no doubt you're aware of most of it. I want to share something that has some small potential to be helpful. We have learned of a potential weakness that this thing has. It might be vulnerable to a very specific type of attack. Do you understand?"

"Yes, Mr. President."

"It has some sort of plating on the side. That is what protects it from everything we've thrown at it so far."

"We hit it with our Howitzer, but did no apparent damage, sir." Jayden said.

"There you go. Here's the good news. Those plates can open. That is how it builds up pressure for an attack. When it does so, it is possible that it could be harmed by an attack from the rear. They hinge at the front, open at the back—you see?"

"Yes, Mr. President."

"The problem is getting a weapon of some sort and a crew to operate it directly behind the monster at the exact time it builds pressure for an attack, without getting discovered or destroyed by this thing."

Jayden exchanged a glance with Withers. "We read you, Mr. President."

"The whole process has presented many issues to us as we've tried to come up with a practical operational plan. I've been consulting with some experts back here in the White House (the six Marines had trouble not smiling a little at that), and we've identified a multitude of roadblocks. Let me ask you this—do you have any sort of weapon with you?"

"Yes, sir. We brought some SAM's along."

"Excellent! Do you think you could get behind this thing if you had to?

Jayden didn't want to say anything negative, but he had doubts. "It's hard to follow. It moves very fast, and leaves a trail of wreckage in the way. So far, Mr. President, we haven't even been able to catch up to it."

"I want you to try. Those are your new marching orders. Get behind it, and we'll come up with some sort of distraction for the front. When it stops to attack, you can blast it from behind. Can you two manage that, son?"

There was only one answer. "Yes, sir!"

"We'll do our part. Stay in contact. Good hunting, men."

Withers stopped the car in the middle of the road.

"What are you doing, Staff Sergeant?" Jayden asked.

"How are we going to get behind that thing?"

"What do you mean, sir?"

"The only time we even got close was when it came ashore. We've been driving after it for hours and not making any progress. We can't track it. Shit, we don't know when it turns, or stops, or reverses itself. We don't know where it is even now. How are we ever going to establish a position directly behind it?"

Jayden didn't have an answer.

"And just as bad, how are they going to get a target in front of it at the moment we're ready to shoot? That thing can destroy its enemies from miles away. How did it know where our firing position was when it wiped us out? It must have hit us from what…three miles away?"

"At least, Sergeant."

Withers rubbed the stubble on his face while he thought. "We need a plan, Davis. Shit luck isn't going to do it."

"Yes, sir."

"I've got nothing. I need your help."

Jayden had no idea what to do. "I'm not sure how much help I'm going to be, Staff Sergeant."

"Look, Davis. Driving around in this car isn't going to get it done. I need you to think. I know how smart you are—use it! There's got to be some way of getting behind that thing. We'll let the others figure the frontal part out for themselves."

Jayden felt overwhelmed. There were more obstacles than answers by far. What to do?

"Come on, Private. This is your chance to impress me."

Jayden frowned. "It's more than that. It's life and death for millions of people."

"Yeah, I know. No pressure."

Jayden fought to clear his mind. "Okay, let's start with this. Do you like steak?"

Withers gave him a skeptical look. "What?"

"Do you like steak? A nice sirloin, maybe. With fried mushroom and onions."

"Sure do. But that seems just a little off topic, Davis."

Jayden shook his head. "Maybe not. You and I both love steaks, but neither of us would try to eat it in one huge bite. Correct?"

"Affirmative. Not unless you wanted to have some restaurant patron perform the Heimlich maneuver on you."

"Exactly. You eat it one bite at a time."

"What's your point, Davis?"

"We're looking at one, gigantic issue. Let's try breaking it down into bite sized pieces. Maybe that will help."

Withers didn't look sold. "What's your idea of a bite sized piece?"

"What's the first thing we have to do if this is going to happen?"

Withers shrugged. "Get behind it, like we just said."

"No. That's almost the very last thing. First figure out how to track it. Then get close. Then find a way to sneak in behind it. Coordinate all that with the frontal distraction that will make it go into attack mode."

"Simple."

"Forget everything except the tracking issue for now," Jayden said. "That's step one."

"Fine. That's a big enough piece anyway. And frankly, I don't have any good ideas."

Jayden shook his head. "Forget "good" ideas. This is the brainstorming phase of our plan, which means any idea is good, no matter how ridiculous it sounds. So with that in mind, do you have any thoughts at all—even ones that seem silly?"

Withers scowled. "I don't even like the word "silly". How about "impractical"?"

Jayden nodded. "Whatever. Sure. Give me an impractical idea if you've got one."

"All right," Withers said. "How about this? They get one of the military satellites to track this thing. Then all the wreckage doesn't matter. Neither does the speed it's moving or any maneuvers it tries to pull."

Jayden beamed. "That's a great idea, Staff Sergeant! Why did you think it was so impractical?"

"Because you don't fly a satellite like a plane. It takes a while to get it in position, it stays there for a limited amount of time, and can only see when viewing conditions are ideal...which they are not. Between fog and the smoke and dust from the destruction...I just don't know if it would be worth the effort. Besides, if we sit around and wait, then find out it isn't working...we're screwed."

Jayden looked up at the sky, partially covered by thin, wispy clouds. "Man, I hate to give up on that idea. Imagine having an eye in the sky. That would help us so…" His voice trailed off.

"Davis? Are you all right?"

"Yeah." His voice was quiet, unfocused.

"Well, what is it then?" Withers asked.

"What else can be used for aerial surveillance besides satellites?"

Withers had a vision of a blimp drifting towards them, which was useless. "I don't know, Davis. We don't have time for guessing games."

"What about a drone?"

Withers snapped back to attention. "Yeah. Now that might work. The problem is the time it would take to get one here, and preventing the monster from blowing it out of the sky."

Jayden saw where he was going. "No, Staff Sergeant. Not a military drone. What about a small, civilian drone? Something the monster wouldn't even notice. Something we should be able to find in any electronics store. They come with cameras. They can fly hundreds, if not thousands of feet in the air. A decent one should work perfectly."

"Shit." Withers now sported a smile. "See, I tried to tell you that you're the brains of the outfit. I don't suppose there's any chance you've flown one of these things before?"

"You bet your ass I have…sir."

"In that case, I think we just chewed up the first bite sized piece of our mission. Let's see if we can find one and get it to work. I'll drive, you give directions."

Jayden pulled out his phone, searching for electronics stores. "Let's go."

A short time later, Jayden was stepping away from a four engine drone that had been placed in the abandoned parking lot outside the store where they had made their purchase. He tried to familiarize himself with the controls.

"I can't believe that guy insisted that we pay," Withers said. He had been surprised that there was even anybody working. "Here we are on the brink of complete destruction and he's worried about making a buck. Good thing you carry your credit card even on duty."

Jayden could imagine people doing worse things than selling stuff just before the apocalypse unfolded. "This controller is different than the one I used before."

Withers knew he would be of no help. "Can you fly it?"

The small propellers on top of the drone spun to life, emitting a high pitched whine.

"I believe so, Staff Sergeant. Here, take my phone."

The display on the cell phone would relay the image from the camera on the drone. The Sergeant held it in one beefy hand. "Now what?"

"Just touch it anywhere on the screen. That should bring it up."

"Umm…"

"What's wrong, Sergeant."

"It's a picture."

"Really? Just close it."

"It's somebody's boobs."

Jayden felt himself blush. "Just close it, sir."

"Okay, that's better. I can see the grass under the drone."

"Right. Here we go."

The engines grew louder as the drone lifted, with a little wobble. Jayden raised it to around twenty feet, so he'd have room for error if he got into trouble with the controls. Soon it was hovering, holding steady.

"It's not as bad as I thought it might be, Sergeant. I'm going to take it up."

"Do it."

The drone leapt skyward. Its momentum was impressive. Soon it was just a speck.

"How's that, sir? See anything?"

Withers frowned. "Yeah. The city is a mess. No sign of the monster yet."

"I'll go higher." Jayden worked the controls.

"Wait! Got it!"

Jayden tried to level the drone. "Where?"

Withers gathered his bearings. "Almost due east, I think." He pointed with his finger. "That way. Maybe, I don't know…a mile and a half?"

"Funny we haven't heard it for a while."

Withers considered the course it seemed to be taking. "You know what? It might be headed back to the waterfront."

Jayden felt a chill. "Shit. We might not have much time, Staff Sergeant."

"Yeah. But at least we know where it is. Let's get moving. We'll try to head it off. You call in and let headquarters know what's going on."

When the call came in, the President took it. "Hey, quiet down! Shut up, all of you!"

The room grew silent.

"Go ahead. I read you loud and clear."

"This is PFC Davis, sir. I just wanted to give you an update."

"Outstanding, Davis. What's happening on your end?"

"We are tracking the monster, sir. We think we can head it off and make contact."

"My God, that's phenomenal! How are you doing that?"

"We're using a small civilian drone, sir."

The Commander-in-Chief pumped his fist in the air. "There, you see? That's what I'm talking about. How's that for ingenuity? Tell me son, where is the monster now?"

"It's in the central part of the city, moving southward."

"Okay. Now listen to me. We have a plan. At this very moment, there is a high speed boat with Navy Seals loading onto it just offshore. They are going to come in, then coordinate with you on where to ambush this thing. Do you understand?"

"Yes, sir. I believe so, sir. How long until the Seals make shore?"

The President consulted before answering. "They're just getting ready to launch from the USS Trent, which is currently eight miles offshore. They should arrive in approximately thirty minutes, maybe longer depending on wave conditions."

The radio went silent.

"What is it, Davis? Can you still hear me?"

"Sir, we believe the monster may be heading back to the waterfront. We also think it likely, based on what you just said, that it will reach there before the Marines land. If that's the case, they'll be sitting ducks, Mr. President."

The President looked at the ceiling, taking a moment to compose himself. "Damn it! How sure are you of this, Davis?"

"We can't be certain, Mr. President. But as of this moment, that's where it's headed."

"All right, fine. You keep tracking it. Let us fine tune our plan. We'll be in touch. And by the way, good work—both of you."

Aya had regained enough focus to resume working. Talking with the President had thrown off his concentration. After settling a minor domestic disturbance, he returned to the office to do paperwork. There was still significant interest in the television feed of the San Francisco attack. Aya wanted to watch, but figured he'd been off task enough already for this day.

"Corporal, can I see you in my office?"

That didn't take long, Aya thought to himself.

Sergeant Taft waved him into the chair while he closed the door. Taft walked around his desk, sat, musing.

"What's up, Sarge?" Aya figured he would break the ice, helping to get whatever this was over with. Verbal reprimand was his best guess at this point.

"Look, Aya, I was pretty tough on you earlier. I've had time to think about it, and have come to the conclusion that I was…embarrassed to be associated with your plan. You had me way out of my comfort zone. That's why I was so adamant not to encourage you or get involved in any way."

"All things considered, that seems like a normal reaction to something as crazy as what I was suggesting," Aya said.

"No, it was a poor response by a superior officer. I should have been more accommodating. Or at the very least, I should have allowed you to elaborate on all the details before making my decision. So…I apologize."

Aya nodded. "Thank you. I accept."

Taft looked puzzled. "You took that well."

Aya shrugged.

Taft stared hard before continuing. "You did something, didn't you? After I told you not to, you went out that door and started calling people against my orders."

"That is a possibility," Aya said.

Taft sat back in his chair, rolling his eyes. "You son of a bitch. Who'd you call? The Governor, I suppose. Should I expect an e-mail suggesting that one of my officers needs to have a psychiatric assessment?"

"If you do, it's going to come from the White House."

Taft jumped as if slapped. "Very funny. I assume you're trying to cultivate a sense of humor now as a way of defusing tense situations."

The expression on Aya's face remained impassive. He offered no further explanation.

"Please tell me you didn't call the White House," Taft said, his voice dropping as his concern rose.

"I can't do that, Bill."

Taft looked to be in physical pain. "But only to a secretary or receptionist, right?"

Aya met his gaze but said nothing.

"An executive assistant?"

It was time to end this, Aya decided. "I spoke to the President."

Taft, all the way to the expression on his face, froze in position. "You did not."

"For what it's worth, he seemed very interested in the information I shared."

The color in Taft's face had drained. "About your dream?"

"My vision."

Taft, in a gesture of complete resignation, bent down to the extent his forehead almost touched his desk. "You know the men wearing white coats are on their way here to throw a net over you even as we speak, right?"

Aya didn't seem upset by the pronouncement. "I do not think so. The White House seemed quite preoccupied by the attack."

Taft looked back up. "Yeah, there is still that."

"Bill," Aya said, "I haven't heard any updates since this morning. Do you know what's happening in San Francisco?"

Taft shook his head. "Not really. The military isn't releasing any information and the media is speculating to fill in the gaps. All I can tell you is, so far, there hasn't been any good news."

Aya frowned. "I am sorry to hear that."

Taft was struggling to reconnect with reality, moving on from his concerns about the fall-out from the White House call. "You're not the only one." He stood up. "Hell, we might as well go watch the news for a while. I'm going to get fired after your little stunt anyway."

Aya opened the door for both of them. "You'll be fine, Bill. Trust me."

Taft pointed a finger as he walked past. "If you say that you learned that in a dream, I'll shoot you right here and now."

Aya walked out behind him, a smile across his face.

17

They were on open roads now. The Beemer was flying. The plan dictated that they had to get to the waterfront before the monster did. Otherwise, the possibility came into play that it would go back into the water and disappear. If that happened, another random attack seemed both likely and unpreventable. So far, nobody had been able to track it underwater.

"Should we stop and check on its movements, Staff Sergeant?" Jayden said.

"Negative. I want to get to the waterfront first. We'll assume the worst and focus on cutting it off. Once we get there, if we find out its changed course and is still moving around the city itself, then we'll know we have some time for an ambush elsewhere."

"Yes, sir."

"Hey, Davis. Your phone must have GPS. Bring it up and tell me how much further we have to go."

They crested a hill at high speeds, the expensive sedan's suspension smoothing the maneuver.

"No need, Staff Sergeant. See that?"

In the distance, a small slice of blue water was now visible at the end of the road.

"Perfect! Hold on." Withers pressed even harder on the accelerator.

"If we're going to die today, Staff Sergeant, I'd rather it wasn't from a car accident."

"Relax. Two minutes, we'll be there. Get on the horn and let somebody know we're almost in position."

"Yes, sir," Jayden said, thankful for a distraction from the reckless speed they were going.

The energy was starting to drain from the Situation Room. After hours of frantic planning and monitoring results, discouragement was beginning to sneak in to the mindsets of those gathered there. Nothing they had tried thus far had yielded any positive results.

"Mr. President?"

Reynolds walked over and stood, waiting his reply.

"Well, you've got balls, Lieutenant Major, I'll give you that much. What is it?"

"The next wave is now approaching the city."

"Which is what?"

"Predator drones, A-10's and the fast attack ship USS Warwick, sir. She is carrying Tomahawks with special warheads should you choose to want that as an option."

"What about those marines?"

"We were waiting for your authorization before sending them in, sir."

Another person, wearing a decorated military uniform, approached.

"Everything happens at once. Now what is it?" The President scowled.

"The radio, sir. A call is coming in from those artillery troops."

Now the Commander-in-Chief seemed energized. "Great. I'll take it. Reynolds, you wait right there."

Jayden relayed his version of good news as soon as the President came on line. However this was going to work out, it was going to happen soon, and that was making him nervous.

"Outstanding!" the President said after learning that they were nearly in position. He had to make a decision now. "I'm going to release the Seal Team. We'll put you in direct radio contact so you can coordinate with them as they approach." He turned to Reynolds. "Make it happen, Lieutenant Major."

"Yes, sir." He scurried off with his orders.

"Listen to me, PFC Davis. As much as I want to, I can't tell you what to do. This is going to require spur of the moment, on-site decisions on your part, and on the Seal Team's part. Do you understand?"

"Yes, Mr. President. I'll leave the decision making to my CO."

"Chain of command is important, son. But if you get any bright ideas, you speak up. This is no time for pulling rank. We're all in this up to our necks. If someone comes up with a viable idea on how to defeat this thing, I don't give a rat's ass what his or her rank is. Is that clear?"

"Yes, sir. Clear, Mr. President."

"Good. I'll have the Team leader call you as soon as they launch. Am I to assume this thing is still moving towards the water?"

"Yes, sir. As far as we know."

"How long until it reaches the water?"

Davis had no motivation to speak anything but the truth. "Soon. Probably within the next ten minutes or so, Mr. President, unless it stops or changes direction."

The Commander-in-Chief winced at the bad news.

"Listen to me, Davis. First of all, what's your first name?"

"Uh, Jayden, sir."

"Jayden, I'm not going to sugar coat this. Based on the time line you have estimated, the Seal Team will not arrive in time to intercept this thing before it reaches the water. Not even close. We now have more assets within striking distance, but that didn't work before so why would it now? I can authorize a strike with our most devastating weapons, but I'm loath to do that. If the monster destroys us, that's one thing. We will not destroy ourselves."

Jayden thought he understood the implications. "Yes, sir."

"At this point, based on what little I do know, I think the time has arrived to admit temporary defeat. You two find some shelter and get out of its way. If we have time—if it hesitates or turns back around—then we'll coordinate something. If it heads straight for the water, which is what I expect it to do, we'll regroup to figure out a better plan of attack for the next time it appears. Do you read me?"

"I read you, Mr. President."

"Thank you for your assistance and courage under difficult circumstances, PFC Davis. Good luck to you both. Be safe."

"Yes, sir."

The call ended. The President gazed around the now quiet room.

"God help us all."

The sedan screamed to a stop as they reached the last intersection before the water's edge. Withers hesitated, then shut off the engine.

Jayden had no idea what came next. "What now, Staff Sergeant?"

Withers had heard the conversation with the President. "I don't know. I guess we'd better find some cover before that thing gets here."

They both stepped out of the Beemer, looking around. Despite everything that had transpired, this part of the waterfront was still beautiful.

"What about one of those warehouses?" Withers asked.

They looked flimsy to Jayden. The monster could crush them without trying. "I suppose so, Staff Sergeant. This would be easier if we had a better idea where it was going to come out."

Withers looked over his shoulder in the direction they had just come. "Let's put that drone up one more time. Maybe we can pinpoint its exact course."

"Yes, sir." Jayden grabbed it and the controller from the car. He wasted no time in sending it skyward. He didn't know how long until the monster would appear on the horizon, and he didn't want to waste any time.

"See anything, Sergeant?"

"Yeah. Hold your position. Let me get my bearings again."

Jayden levelled the drone, letting it hover.

"Shit. You know what?" Withers locked eyes with Jayden. "It's coming right at us. I think it's on the exact same street. I wonder if it was somehow tracking our movement. We've got to get out of here and fast."

Jayden started to bring the drone back down.

"Hurry up, Davis. I'm not kidding. We don't have much time."

Jayden, now very nervous, brought the drone down too fast, crashing it into pieces on the roadway.

"Damn!"

"Forget it!" Withers yelled. "Let's go!"

"What about the SAM's?" Jayden asked.

"Uh…shit. All right. Let's each grab one. But do it fast!"

"You have the keys, Sergeant. Pop the trunk."

The lid lifted leisurely, as if there was no need to rush at all.

Jayden got there first, reaching in to grab one. It was heavy, and he strained to lift it out.

"Great. Now get out of my way," Withers snarled.

The Sergeant was more flustered than Jayden had ever seen before. He took a step back, feeling his feet land on the rigid lid of a manhole cover. Part of his mind went blank as the rest went into overdrive.

"All right. Let's go!"

Jayden stood motionless.

"Davis, did you hear me?"

He looked around, regaining his concentration. "Yes, sir."

"Then come on!"

Jayden didn't move.

"Davis, what the hell is wrong with you?"

"Sarge, can I ask you something?"

"For fuck's sake Davis! Make it fast!"

"Can you change a tire?"

"Davis? Do I need to throw you over my shoulder?"

"No, sir. Do you think there's a spare and a jack under this cover?"

Withers gritted his teeth. "I'm sure there is, but this is a real bad time for you to lose your shit."

"Could you use the jack to lift this manhole cover off?"

Withers looked at it, not comprehending. "Seriously?"

Jayden nodded. "Yes, sir. I have an idea, sir."

Withers looked around, still seeing no signs of the monster's approach. Regardless, they had little time. "Do you think you could explain and make it *real* quick?"

Jayden smiled. "Yes, sir."

They were one full block back from the waterfront. How they had made it this far without the monster catching them, Jayden had no idea. To top it off, the manhole cover had been a bitch.

The two of them, straining to their limits, had barely been able to get it loose. Jayden guessed it hadn't been off in a while. The sound of something huge moving through the city reached their ears as it popped open. They wasted no time in sliding it away, exposing the opening.

"Get in there, Davis!"

The smell emitting from the dark hole wasn't encouraging. There could be no doubt what was causing it. "Right, Sarge." There was no time for second thoughts.

"You sure you can manage the SAM in there?"

Only Jayden's head now remained above ground. "Yes, sir. I'll find a way."

Withers handed it to him, looking doubtful. Jayden maneuvered it in an effort to get a sufficient grip; his back pressing against the wall of the manhole was the only thing keeping him from falling. "Is that even going to fit down there?"

Sounds of destruction were getting louder. Jayden swore the ground was starting to vibrate. "Just go! Do what you've got to do, sir, or it's going to be too late for both of us."

Withers took one last reluctant look, then ran full out, back towards the water.

"Okay," Jayden said to himself and the invisible force of destiny that seemed to envelope him. Now that the plan was unfolding, getting the missile in the hole seemed more difficult that he had imagined. And that was with gravity working with him. Lifting it back out of the narrow opening might be impossible. There were seconds left to come up with an alternate idea, but his mind was filled with a fear induced fog.

Life or death, success or failure…it all hinged on what transpired in the next couple of minutes.

Then the monster roared.

The cry of the monster almost threw Withers off of his feet. It was excruciating to endure. It sounded like there was a chalkboard against the side of his head and someone was dragging metal talons along the surface, only so much louder. He gritted his teeth, forcing himself to continue towards the car. Despite his renewed focus, he couldn't help but glance back over his shoulder.

The monster was now in full view. It was disgusting in so many ways, but it was real and moving straight towards him. The size was unimaginable...huge to the point where it barely fit down the street without being jammed against the buildings on either side. It moved forward crushing everything in its path with apparent ease. Withers looked for an instant, (tripping and falling now would have disastrous consequences), but couldn't see any signs of Davis. Hopefully he was safely ensconced in the sewer, somehow surviving the passing of this unimaginable horror as it went over his head.

Withers made a right turn just before reaching the Beemer, pressing the panic button on the key chain as he ran past. The horn blared, and the lights flashed. A separate siren added additional noise, and Withers hoped it would both grab the monster's attention, and motivate it to stop and attack. It seemed that was their only hope. He dashed over the sidewalk and into the door of a coffee shop for some cover.

He stopped, breathing deep, watching to see the monster's reaction.

Jayden made a decision. He left the SAM on the ground beside the manhole opening. There was no way he could get it down the hole, then back up in time to fire it at the monster. He could only hope and pray that somehow the enormous beast wouldn't step on it, destroying it. If it did, this plan became useless in an instant.

He climbed all the way down the ladder, less concerned about what lay at the bottom than what was about to pass overhead. The walls vibrated around him. He wondered if the monster would be heavy enough to collapse the sewer walls on top of him. He stepped off into shallow "water" and stood waiting. It didn't take long.

The monster passed overhead. The sun was blocked out, the darkness inside the sewer, total. Jayden was sure he heard small pieces of something falling off the walls and ceiling into the water. The ground rumbled under the strain, and to top it off, the monster's cry was deafening.

It was muffled because he was underground, but that didn't change the hideous, otherworldly nature of it. Jayden refocused, preparing to implement the final stage of his plan. If Sarge could get this thing to stop and attack, there was a slim chance he could get off a shot at the open plates. If not, then the monster would be free to continue its rampage of unlimited carnage.

Despite the stench, hunkering in the sewer, (as opposed to being up there where it was), seemed like a good idea.

The monster kept coming. And it was moving fast. Why wasn't it attacking the car? Withers winced. In a few seconds, it would be past him, no doubt crushing the car as it went. Then the plan was a failure.

"Fuck it." Withers grabbed the SAM that was on the ground beside him, stepping back outside. There was no time to consider the consequences.

"Hey!" he screamed at the black behemoth, not even knowing if that would get its attention. He whipped the missile into firing position on his shoulder, doing what he had been trained to do.

The SAM fired, the missile streaking out of the tube towards the face on the monster. Withers watched with some satisfaction as it zeroed in, then struck the target. The missile exploded, spewing smoke and flame as the sound echoed along the street.

The monster stopped. Now he had its full and undivided attention.

Great.

Sunlight once again flooded down from the cover opening. Jayden knew any chance of success would depend on split second timing. He sprang into action, climbing the ladder as fast as he could, despite misgivings about the vulnerable position he would be putting himself in.

He scrambled out, looked up, and saw the monster moving away— but still very close. Then the sound of an explosion, and the great beast stopped. Sarge must have shot it! Do or die, this was the moment. He lifted the SAM with some difficulty, but got it into firing position nonetheless. Determination was a wonderful motivator.

Now, if only the plates would open.

He tried to site in, but his angle wasn't good. He was too directly behind it to get a good shot at the plates even if they did open. He stepped to the side, careful to maintain good footing.

"Come on, you bastard. Open up."

Withers had completed two thirds of his mission. He had the monster's attention, and he had managed to get the gigantic beast to stop. Only one thing remained.

Knowing full well he couldn't do any real damage, he still decided to utilize the one remaining option for irritating the beast. He drew his .45, taking aim at its head.

"Suck on this!" he screamed. He pulled the trigger, firing off a round. He couldn't see the results, but with a target this huge, he was confident that he had scored a hit. He fired another.

"Come on, you pussy! Fight back!" He fired off several more shots.

The monster wanted to get into the water. It now had a secret. Instinctively, it sensed that a transformation was about to occur. It had reached the size and stage of development where it was going to go through a metamorphosis. Once in a safe place, it would molt its outer skin, emerging as a different creature. One that was larger and more dangerous. One that could settle in and overpower this planet. One that could fulfil its destiny. Once that was accomplished, reproduction would come next; followed by total domination.

Neither the bullets nor the missile that had previously struck it had done any serious harm. But, it had been hit multiple times, and continued to be hit, and that was sufficient to annoy and concern the monster.

It would eliminate this threat, then move back into the water. Under the cover provided by the Pacific Ocean, the larval stage could finish, and the monster would move on to bigger and better things.

It settled in to a good position, preparing to attack.

Withers saw it happen, knowing he had fulfilled his part of the mission as best as he could. But now what? Odds of success were impossible to estimate, because he didn't know anything about this monster. *Too late to turn back now*, he thought. Then he saw the plates loosen and move for the first time.

Jayden saw it too. The first movement was just a release of sorts, a relaxation of the muscles that held the massive plates in position; not an outright opening. He forced himself to concentrate, loosening the pressure of his finger on the trigger. If he fired too soon, this chance evaporated. It was a one shot deal.

The plates moved again. This time there was no doubt what was happening. It was elating and terrifying all at once to know that his potential opportunity was about to present itself, but the movement of the plates would also herald the firing of the monsters main weapon.

Timing was everything. The huge plates pivoted open, but only in transition. They closed again in a rhythmic pattern. Jayden wasn't sure when to pull the trigger. Too soon, or too late, and the SAM would hit the outer portion of the plates and explode harmlessly. As far as that went, even if he did strike a perfect hit, he wasn't sure if this gargantuan freakish creature would be seriously hurt. He wanted to think this out, but time was wasting.

There would be a delay while he pulled the trigger.

There would be a delay while the weapon discharged.

There would be a delay while it flew through the air towards the target.

The plates were moving, perhaps even faster now. How many more cycles until the monster was charged and ready to fire? Freezing in place until the opportunity passed was the ultimate failure, Jayden decided.

Open, shut. Open, shut. Open...

Jayden allowed a brief prayer to flicker through his mind, then pulled the trigger.

The missile did what it was supposed to do, firing and streaking away, towards its target.

"Come on!" Jayden screamed.

The plates closed and were in the process of reopening. Had he fired too soon? The missile reached the monster as they started to gape, barely slipping past the massive plate, penetrating the less protected insides. For the briefest of moments, Jayden started to think it had misfired, or that the soft guts wouldn't be enough to detonate the warhead.

And then it exploded. It was a disappointing, muffled pop. That was all. No massive, destructive blast, like he had been hoping for. But appearances can be deceiving.

The bladder which held the massive buildup of pressure had been damaged by the blast. It held for several seconds while the monster tried to process what had just happened. Then the laws of physics kicked in, and the bladder lost the battle. The air pressure released in a sudden, violent burst.

Jayden watched in awe as one of the giant plates flew off of the monster, and its body exploded outward. Pieces of flesh and other parts were launched in all directions in a disgusting burst of gore. The monster gave a hideous, ear piercing shriek, even as parts of it started to land all around. It toppled, crushing the sides of the buildings as it went. It landed with a massive thud, and lay twitching as greyish liquid oozed out of the wound. The smell made the sewer seem like fresh flowers.

Realization crept in. Jayden smiled, pumping his fist. "Yes!"

The body and parts blown off of it covered the street. That was a problem because there was one last question to answer. Had Withers survived the ordeal? If so, how could he get to him to render aid if needed?

"Sarge!"

Withers couldn't tell what was happening behind the beast. He braced himself for the impact of the attack in case any one of the hundreds of things that could go wrong did.

He saw it hesitate while the plates were in the open position, thought briefly to himself that it was a good sign. Then, the monster exploded.

It was wonderful to behold, until a large, wet piece of its rent flesh hit him, knocking him to the ground, unconscious.

Jayden made his way through the mess. Stinking hunks of grey, wet meat the size of compact cars created a maze of horror and revulsion. This might have been better than getting killed by the monster, but not by much. Despite his conviction not to do so, (and his very best efforts to prevent it), Jayden hunched over, vomiting.

"Oh God, that's awful." The moisture from the oozing hunks was starting to soak through his clothes, adding a new layer of disgust to his response. He would have to shower for hours to get this off. His uniform would be burnt or buried, never to be worn again. He needed to refocus his attention away from the smell and feel of his environment.

"Sarge! Are you there?" He slogged forward, every movement an effort in self-control. There was no response.

There, in front of him, was a solid wall of monster flesh. Disgusted, he knew he would have to either climb over it, or push it out of the way. The very thought of it took him to the limits of his inner strength. He knew if he hesitated, it was over.

"Come on, Jayden. You can do this."

Withers was coming back to full consciousness. He felt an innate urge to take a deeper breath. He sucked in a small piece of something that tasted so horrible, he was shocked awake. He spit it out, gagging.

"There you are. Not so tasty, is it?"

Withers looked up at PFC Davis' smiling face. He continued to spit, unable to get the rancid taste out of his mouth.

"Help me up," he ordered between expectorations.

Jayden was happy to comply, extended a helping hand. "You might as well barf and get it over with. It helps a little."

Withers regained his feet, working on maintaining his balance. "Shit! That is disgusting." He unbuttoned his camo shirt at the top, reached inside, withdrawing a small flask.

"Staff Sergeant! That doesn't look like regulation Army equipment."

Withers took a good, long swig, then lowered the flask while grimacing. "No, but it helps."

"In that case..." Jayden extended his hand. Withers gave him a funny look, then handed over the flask. He turned his attention to the carcass of the monster.

"You did it Davis. Son of a bitch!" A huge smile crossed his face.

Jayden swallowed a mouthful of straight whiskey, trying not to gag. "*We* did it, Sarge."

The burly officer grabbed Jayden in an impromptu bear hug. "My God, Davis! I'm going to recommend that you get promoted to Five Star General!"

"I appreciate it, Sarge. Just don't break any ribs, okay?"

Withers released him. "You are one fine soldier, son. I can't think of anybody else who could have maintained their composure through that kind of fuckery. What a shot that must have been."

"Just between you and me, no matter what I say in all the interviews, it was sheer, dumb luck."

"Oh, I don't think so." Withers blew out a long breath of air, while staring at what was left of the monster. "You know what? We'd better call somebody with the good news before they decided to nuke the city or something along those lines."

"Yes, sir," Jayden agreed. This would be by far the best call of the day.

"Mr. President? It's a radio call for you, sir."

The President looked tired. "Well, unless you can think of a better idea, patch me through."

"Yes, sir."

A voice, exuberant in tone and significant in volume, blared out of the speaker. "Mr. President, are you there?"

"I'm here. Is this PFC Davis?"

"Yes, sir. Alive and well."

"That's encouraging. What's the situation on the ground, son?" asked the Command-in-Chief without any real hope that the news would be good.

"We did it, Mr. President! The monster is dead!"

The situation room was silent.

"Say that again, Davis."

"It's dead, sir. We killed it."

It was a wonderful statement, but it was also hard to believe.

"Listen to me, Davis," the President said. "I want you to explain. What do you mean? Give me details."

"We did what you said, sir. I got behind it; the Sarge got in front. He distracted it, goading it into attacking. I waited until the plates were open and shot it with the SAM. After that, the whole thing just exploded." It was a gross over-simplification—but still sounded awesome.

The President looked around. "Get me a fly by with an AWAKs or chopper...or whatever. I want confirmation." The room once again became a flurry of activity. "That's the best news I've heard in a long time, Davis. At the risk of being insulting, are you absolutely sure?"

"Yes, sir. I'm looking at what's left of it right now."

"Do you have a phone, Davis?"

"I do, sir."

"Here's my personal number. Only celebrities and heads of state have it, but don't worry about that right now. Take a photo and send it to me." He recited the digits.

"Yes, sir."

Less than a minute later, the President was staring at the screen on his cell.

"That's a hell of a mess, but he's right. I think they did it."

Cheering broke out around the room. The President waved everybody back to silence.

"Davis, are you two all right? Are you injured in any way?"

"I don't think so. The Sarge might have a minor head injury." Jayden noticed light bleeding from where his head had hit the street when knocked down.

"Listen to me. Get to a safe place and don't move. The Calvary is on the way. We'll get you out of there ASAP. Do you understand?"

"Yes, sir. I believe we're safe now."

"Outstanding. Let me speak to your Sergeant."

Withers took the radio. "This is Withers, Mr. President."

"Outstanding work, Staff Sergeant. Or should I say, Major."

"Sir?"

"I'm of the opinion that a small promotion is in order. Everyone else here is in agreement with me, or they will be shortly. How does that sound?"

"I…was thinking about retirement, Mr. President."

"Fine. There's nothing wrong with that. Retiring as a Major should help the pension, correct?"

"Yes, sir."

"That settles that. Now you two stay safe. We'll get you out of there very soon."

"Thank you, Mr. President."

Withers put the radio down, looking stunned.

Aya knew it was well past the end of his shift, but couldn't pull himself away from the office. Or more precisely, the news feed on the television.

Somehow the monster had been destroyed. Details were sketchy and inconsistent, but an overhead shot from a chopper showed the ruined body of the thing laying in what was left of the street. Aya marvelled at the sheer size of it, wondering if it was in fact the same creature that had ravaged their villages.

Sergeant Taft was standing beside him. Aya hadn't noticed him approach.

"Thank God that's over."

Aya nodded but got interrupted before he could respond.

"Corporal Chee," their dispatcher said. "There's a call for you."

"Thanks Nancy." Aya took the call at his desk. "Yes, Corporal Chee speaking."

"Corporal!" The booming voice could only belong to one person. After all, it wasn't like this was the first time they had a conversation over the phone.

"Hello, Mr. President."

There were four people in the station, the other three now had their full and undivided attention now focused on his every word.

"Listen, I just wanted to make sure you didn't get left out in all the excitement. I assume by now you've heard the good news."

"Yes, sir. I'm watching coverage right now."

"I passed on your suggestion to our folks on the ground. They used it, and it worked! Without that guidance, we would no doubt still be fighting this thing. So, on behalf of the American people, as well as myself, I want to say thank you."

"I'm glad I was able to help."

"I want you to give your personal contact information to the nice lady who is going to come on the line. You are going to get an invitation to Washington very soon, and I expect you will accept."

"Yes, Mr. President."

"It's going to involve a lot of fanfare, hand shaking, crowds applauding and all that sort of thing."

Aya winced. "Yes, sir. Whatever you say."

"I know, I know. It's going to be a pain in the ass. But let me ask you this. What kind of fishing do you have up there in your part of the state?"

"We have excellent fishing, sir."

"Good. Then once the pomp and circumstance is over, I'm going to go on an official visit to Alaska. You can catch a ride with me, if that suits you."

Riding on Air Force One? "If you insist, sir."

"I do. Then you can take me on an unofficial fishing excursion. What do you say?"

"I'd be honored. Perhaps the chief of my tribe should be included."

"Great. Bring along whoever you want. We'll have a blast. I'll put the Secret Service on alert so they can start planning. They love it when I do stuff like this."

Aya could just imagine. "Yes, sir."

"Thank you again, Corporal. We'll be talking soon."

The line clicked and a woman's voice ensued. Aya gave up his personal info, (figuring that they could find him if they wanted to anyway), and hung up. He looked around to discover he had become the center of attention.

Taft was the first to speak. He leaned in close, lowering his voice. "The next time you start talking about some spiritual journey you went on, and I find myself doubting you, I'm going to punch myself in the face."

Aya smiled. "That will not be necessary, Bill. I can do that for you."

He laughed out loud. "Fine. I should know by now that I can trust your judgement."

"Bill, I am tired. I think perhaps tonight will be a better night for sleeping."

Taft nodded. "For a lot of people. Thanks to you."

Aya stood. "I'm going. Oh, by the way, keep your schedule open for a fishing trip in the not too distant future."

"Just you and me?" Taft asked.

"And a few friends. You'll enjoy it, don't worry. And don't doubt me, remember? I'd rather not have to punch you in front of the rest of the staff."

"Go home, Aya. Get some rest."

"Roger that, Sarge." Aya made for the door, trying not to think of the celebrity status that awaited him. He mumbled as he walked.

"Fifteen minutes of fame. Just what I don't need." *No good deed goes unpunished*, he thought. At least a good night's sleep was waiting for him back at the apartment.

That was reward enough.

The End

SEVEREDPRESS

 facebook.com/severedpress
 twitter.com/severedpress

CHECK OUT OTHER GREAT KAIJU NOVELS

MURDER WORLD I KAIJU DAWN
by Jason Cordova
& Eric S Brown

Captain Vincente Huerta and the crew of the Fancy have been hired to retrieve a valuable item from a downed research vessel at the edge of the enemy's space.
It was going to be an easy payday.
But what Captain Huerta and the men, women and alien under his command didn't know was that they were being sent to the most dangerous planet in the galaxy.
Something large, ancient and most assuredly evil resides on the planet of Gorgon IV. Something so terrifying that man could barely fathom it with his puny mind. Captain Huerta must use every trick in the book, and possibly write an entirely new one, if he wants to escape Murder World.

KAIJU ARMAGEDDON
by Eric S. Brown

The attacks began without warning. Civilian and Military vessels alike simply vanished upon the waves. Crypto-zool-ogist Jerry Bryson found himself swept up into the chaos as the world discovered that the legendary beasts known as Kaiju are very real. Armies of the great beasts arose from the oceans and burrowed their way free of the Earth to declare war upon mankind. Now Dr. Bryson may be the human race's last hope in stopping the Kaiju from bringing civilization to its knees.
This is not some far distant future. This is not some alien world. This is the Earth, here and now, as we know it today, faced with the greatest threat its ever known. The Kaiju Armageddon has begun.

SEVEREDPRESS

f facebook.com/severedpress
twitter.com/severedpress

CHECK OUT OTHER GREAT KAIJU NOVELS

KAIJU WINTER
by Jake Bible

The Yellowstone super volcano has begun to erupt, sending North America into chaos and the rest of the world into panic. People are dangerous and desperate to escape the oncoming mega-eruption, knowing it will plunge the continent, and the world, into a perpetual ashen winter. But no matter how ready humanity is, nothing can prepare them for what comes out of the ash: Kaiju!

RAIJU
by K.H. Koehler

His home destroyed by a rampaging kaiju, Kevin Takahashi and his father relocate to New York City where Kevin hopes the nightmare is over. Soon after his arrival in the Big Apple, a new kaiju emerges. Qilin is so powerful that even the U.S. Military may be unable to contain or destroy the monster. But Kevin is more than a ragged refugee from the now defunct city of San Francisco. He's also a Keeper who can summon ancient, demonic god-beasts to do battle for him, and his creature to call is Raiju, the oldest of the ancient Kami. Kevin has only a short time to save the city of New York. Because Raiju and Qilin are about to clash, and after the dust settles, there may be no home left for any of them!

SEVERED**PRESS**

 facebook.com/severedpress
 twitter.com/severedpress

CHECK OUT OTHER GREAT
KAIJU NOVELS

POLAR YETI AND THE BEASTS OF PREHISTORY
by **Matthew Dennion**

A team from Princeton University searching for a lost tribe in Antartica discover a hidden valley filled with wooly mammoths, saber toothed tigers and other Ice Age beasts. Seizing the opportunity of a lifetime, the team set up camp to study the amazing creatures. But there is something else that lives in the Valley. Something terrifying. Something beyond imagination. POLAR YETI!

TITAN WARS
by **M.C. Norris**

Millions of microscopic alien life forms escape a sample canister of water from the frigid depths of outer space. Invisible to the naked eye, a menacing menagerie of more than seventy deadly species react to Earth's warm and fertile seas by launching into metabolic overdrive. Waves of gargantuan abominations begin to rise from the sea, transforming our world into a zoo without cages, where humans plunge to the bottom of the food chain.

In dire need of a zookeeper, the Allied Navy turns to "Psyjack," a bickering geek squad with an outrageous plan to hack into the minds of the megafauna with some reengineered neurosurgical technology. The young gamers hope to level the uneven playing field by fighting monsters with monsters, but they couldn't have anticipated how deadly their technology could be, if it ever fell into the wrong hands ...

www.ingramcontent.com/pod-product-compliance
Lightning Source LLC
Chambersburg PA
CBHW052002170626
46808CB00007B/2735